Avatar

THE MYSTERIES OF
THE SEPTAGRAM

Avatar

THE MYSTERIES OF THE SEPTAGRAM

PAUL BRYERS

Hodder
Children's
Books

A division of Hachette Children's Books

Typeset in Bembo by Avon DataSet Ltd,
Bidford on Avon, Warwickshire

Printed in the UK by CPI Bookmarque, Croydon, CR0 4TD

The paper and board used in this paperback by Hodder Children's Books
are natural recyclable products made from wood grown in sustainable
forests. The manufacturing processes conform to the environmental
regulations of the country of origin.

Hodder Children's Books
a division of Hachette Children's Books
338 Euston Road, London NW1 3BH
An Hachette UK company
www.hachette.co.uk

YA

For Dermot and Elesa

Avatar (noun) from the Sanskrit: meaning 1) the descent of a divine being into the mortal world for a special purpose.

2) an electronic image that represents the player in a computer game.

I seem to move among a world of ghosts
and feel myself the shadow of a dream.
The Princess, ALFRED, LORD TENNYSON

1

The Wolf Child

She lay in bed, suddenly awake and staring into the darkness, wondering what had disturbed her.

Something in the room?

She listened, every nerve taut. Hardly breathing.

Nothing.

But they could be very quiet when they wanted, very still . . . and they didn't have to breathe like she did.

She heard it again.

A wolf.

A wolf, howling in the darkness beyond the castle walls.

She sighed with relief.

Only a wolf.

When she was a little girl – brought up in the city, far from this world of snow and forest and frozen lakes – she used to play at being a wolf. Except that it was something more than play.

'I'm Wolf today,' she would announce at breakfast – and that was it: for the rest of the day she was Wolf. She walked like a wolf, stalked like a wolf, howled like a wolf, even ate like a wolf, when she could get away with it. And the rest of the family had to treat her like a wolf. If they forgot and called her Jade she wouldn't answer them. She just gave them a look – a warning look, with a hint of menace in it, showing her teeth – and they would say, 'Oh, I forgot. You're Wolf today. Sorry.'

And sometimes she would let them off.

Once her Aunt Em asked her, 'Where does Jade go when you're Wolf?'

An interesting question. Jade didn't know. She knew she was in there somewhere, looking out through her wolf eyes, but then, when her Aunt Em got her thinking about it, she wasn't so sure. She imagined that the part of her that was Jade had gone somewhere else for the day, stayed with another family. A family of wolves perhaps. And one of them – a young she-wolf – came to stay with her own family. They swapped for the day.

When she was a bit older she read *The Jungle Book* – the Rudyard Kipling story about Mowgli, the boy who was raised by wolves in India – and her Aunt Em told her there were real children found in India today who had been found living wild in the forest and were covered in bites as if they, too, had been running with the wolf pack. And she told Jade about werewolves – humans who turned into wolves, or thought they did, at the time of the full moon. She said it was a form of mental illness and that there was a medical name for it: lycophobia.

Shortly after this Jade stopped being Wolf, even for a day, because it was too scary thinking you could lose yourself and turn into something else. Something that was certifiably insane.

But she thought about it now as she lay there in the darkness and she thought about her Aunt Em and the rest of her family in London, and when the wolf howled again she felt the loneliness in the sound and she slipped out of bed and padded to the window and looked out over the frozen landscape under its shroud of falling snow. Then she went back to bed and lay awake thinking about her past life and the people she had left behind and the girl she had once been, wondering if she was still there somewhere, buried deep inside her.

She lay awake until dawn, or what passed for dawn in the far northern lands at this time of the year, and a pale grey light seeped into the sky from the other side of the world and she heard the snuffling, questing sounds of a large animal in the corridor outside and the scratching of its long, sharp claws on the wooden panels of her bedroom door.

The beginning of a new day in the Castle of Demons.

2

Missing

'She'll give us Hell for letting them use this,' said
Jade's godmother, the woman she called Aunt Em, as
she brooded over the picture on the front page of the
newspaper. 'If we ever see her again.'

It was the same picture they had used in all the
newspapers, and on all the television channels and on
a hundred different websites: the picture of a young
girl in school uniform with her hair tucked severely
behind her ears and an embarrassed smile – a smile
that said: *I'm only doing this for the camera.*

'I think it's a nice picture,' said Jade's mother
defensively, because it was she who had released it to
the media. Defensive was her normal posture: her
default position, one might say. She was a pale, thin

woman with a long, sharp nose and straggly grey hair. There was no obvious physical resemblance to the girl in the photograph.

Mystery of Missing Jade, said the headline. And the story that followed told how Jade, 'a normal, happy schoolgirl' had gone missing three months earlier in 'mysterious circumstances' after visiting Houndwood Hospital where her godmother, Dr Emily Mortlake, was then working. She had been seen leaving with one of the nurses, a German woman called Sophie Baer-Mellor and neither she nor the nurse had been seen or heard of since.

The 'mysterious circumstances' according to the newspaper were:

1. Houndwood was no ordinary hospital but a hospital for the criminally insane. Why, demanded the newspaper, had an eleven-year-old schoolgirl been allowed anywhere near the place?
2. The nurse appeared to have no family or friends in either England or Germany and had left no traces of her former life.
3. The newspaper could reveal, 'exclusively', that shortly before her disappearance Jade had

learned that she had been adopted – and that the people she thought of as her mother and father were not her real parents at all.

'Who told them?' Emily demanded as she glowered at the newspaper. 'That's what I'd like to know.'

'Well, don't look at me,' said her companion, who had always been more than a little afraid of Emily, even when they were friends at school. But after a moment she said bitterly, 'I always said we should have told her earlier.'

Before Emily could respond to this her mobile phone rang and she fished it out of her handbag and, after glancing to see if she knew the caller, answered with a brisk, 'Yes? Emily Mortlake.'

But then she listened with a gradually deepening frown until finally she said, in her sternest, doctorial voice, 'Just a moment, if you have any information – *any information at all* – I strongly recommend you to go to the police.'

The other woman looked at her sharply.

'Is it about Jade?'

Emily shook her head fiercely and kept her ear glued to the phone.

'I see,' she said. 'Where and when?'

She gestured for pen and paper and wrote down an address.

'Right. I'll see you there.'

She put the phone down and stared blankly into space for a moment. Then she said, 'That was a priest. Sorry, a monk. Brother Benedict. At least that's who he said he was. From Rome.'

'A *monk*? From *Rome*?'

'Yes, they do have monks in Rome, Felicity, and I'm told they walk about quite freely. It's not like an alien from Mars. He said they run some sort of missing persons bureau. Like the Salvation Army, I suppose.'

'So it *was* about Jade? Do they know something?'

'I don't know. I guess I'll find out when we meet.'

'You're going to meet him? In Rome?'

'No. In London. He's coming over specially. He said we should "exchange notes", whatever that means.'

'He might be a nutcase.'

Emily arched her delicate brows.

'We try not to call them that. In the profession. Anyway, he didn't sound like one.'

She gazed out of the window and saw that it was snowing – or trying to; the thin, brittle flakes fluttering at the window like small grey moths, or flakes of ash. A shiver shook her slim shoulders.

'Well, you should at least take someone with you,' her companion insisted.

'No.' Emily shook her head firmly. 'He said to come alone.'

3

The Smelly Bear

Jade opened her bedroom door.

Standing in the passage outside – standing on one leg and scratching at it with the other – was a bear.

'Morning, Laurie,' said Jade. Then she sniffed. 'Is that you?' She wrinkled her nose in disgust.

The bear looked around as if it might be someone else. Jade wasn't fooled.

'My goodness, Laurie, you don't half ronk. You smell like an old bearskin rug.'

The bear took a step backwards and hung its head.

Jade recalled that this was possibly not the kindest thing to say to a living bear, or at least something that closely resembled one.

'Sorry. Didn't mean it. But you've been cooped up

inside for far too long. You need some fresh air. In fact we both need some fresh air.'

There was a note of defiance in her tone. She looked back towards the pale square of light in the window. It didn't seem to be snowing too hard.

'Wait here,' she said, 'while I fetch my cloak.'

4

The Sniper

It had been snowing for three days: a fierce northern snow driven by a wind out of Russia that came howling over the fells like a pack of wolves or an invading army. The two men crouched in their crude shelter on the edge of the frozen lake, listening to the shriek of the wind as it tore through the forest, flaying the tallest trees into submission and burying the smallest under such a weight of snow they looked like strange, misshapen trolls frozen by the breath of Louhi, the Ice Queen.

The men were of the race of *Sami*, hunters and reindeer herders of Lapland, inured to cold and hardship and the long, dark winters of the Arctic Circle. But for three days they had not stirred from the shelter and their minds had begun to play tricks with them so that in the sound of the wind they detected the cries of witches and demons and the many malign spirits of the forest.

The hide was made of branches hacked from the young spruce earlier in the winter and bent into the shape of an igloo, then covered in the skins of reindeer and buried under about a metre of snow. It was almost impossible to detect in the frozen wilderness of lake and fell and forest but the two hunters were taking no chances and would light no fire to keep them warm. Instead they huddled in their survival suits and stamped their fur-lined boots to keep the blood flowing and drank from flasks of hot black tea, laced with *lakka*, the fierce cloudberry liquor of Finland.

From time to time one of them would wriggle on to his stomach and tug at the bindings of a small flap of reindeer skin to expose a thin slit in the side of the shelter a few centimetres above the snowline. At once the wind would tear at this meagre opening with savage teeth and a flurry of snow would rush in like the frozen breath of some monstrous beast. The hunter would press his tinted goggles to the slit and peer through the blizzard sweeping across the frozen lake. Never more than a few seconds, and then he would subside back into his cocoon of fibre and fur with a muttered curse and a shake of the head. For surely nothing mortal could be moving – or living – in that frenzy of whirling snow and ice. And if it was, no mere mortal could see it.

But it was nothing mortal they feared, these hunters; it was something far more frightening. And though their shaman had given them protection against it and the inside of their sanctuary was hung with his spells and charms, they did not entirely trust their value against the unknown power that confronted them across the lake.

And though they were hunters in their everyday lives, now in this dread place they felt that it was they who were the hunted. For this was Lake Piru – the Lake of Demons, legendary gateway of the Nordic Hell. So there was some small comfort in the fury of the storm for surely no one, man nor beast, witch nor demon, could find them out in their lonely haven under its mantle of snow.

But on the morning of the fourth day the wind dropped. And when the elder of the two men, whose name was Issat, the Laughing One, pressed his eyes to the slit and gazed across the frozen lake he saw a darker, grimmer shape emerge from among the dirty rags of cloud that shrouded the distant shore.

The Castle of Demons.

They knew it of old. An ancient keep, long feared by the herders and hunters of the far North; long abandoned to Ghost Owls and other creatures of the dark . . . A place of legend and ill repute. Then, as the clouds shifted, Issat saw something: a movement high on the castle walls, the merest glimpse of red, like a flag fluttering in the wind. He fumbled for his binoculars in their leather case and brought them to his eye, struggling to adjust the focus with his gloved finger.

On one of the towers nearest to the lake was a small figure in a red cloak.

'What is it?' His companion was beside him, his voice harsh with fear. 'What can you see?'

'I think it's her,' murmured Issat. 'The girl.'

Then, as he watched, another figure emerged from the shadows: a dark, inhuman shape almost twice the size of the other. Issat caught his breath and even though he had heard the rumours he could scarce believe his eyes. For it was a bear, a brown bear of the northern forest . . .

But what bear dwelt in a castle and danced to the whim of a child?

Silently he handed the binoculars to his fretful companion and fumbled for the rifle in its waterproof wrappings. He had been trained as a sniper in the Finnish Defence Force and this was a sniper's rifle, a Sako TRG-21, one of the most accurate high-powered rifles in the world, and although Issat was still in the army reserve he had no business to be carrying such a weapon around the forests of Lapland.

He pushed his startled companion aside and slid the gun through the slit in the hide, spreading himself out in the classic sniper's pose, his cheek pressed against the metal stock and his eye to the viewfinder of the powerful night scope.

It was a long shot and in poor light – at the very edge of his skill as a marksman. He framed the red-hooded figure in the crosshairs of the scope, made several slight adjustments to allow for the wind and distance, slipped the safety catch and applied a gentle pressure to the trigger . . .

5

The Fear

The snow swirled around the battlements, dancing a frenzied jig to the mad music of the wind. Jade felt it pushing and pulling at her cloak as if to make her join in − or hurl her down on to the frozen rocks at the foot of the castle walls.

She gripped the wall with one hand and held on to her hood with the other as she peered across the frozen lake. She had seen nothing for days now; nothing but snow. A whiteout so extreme your eyes ached for a shape in the fog, something defined and solid, something real. Something that showed you were still on the same planet; that it hadn't vanished completely, as if wiped out by a giant white rubber leaving you all alone in the vast, lonely, emptiness of space.

But now there was a sudden break in the storm and the veil had lifted to reveal the line of trees at the edge of the lake. Snow-covered, to be sure, but trees for all of that, from a world she had once known but almost forgotten.

And something else.

What was it? Nothing she could see. More a gut feeling: a sense of things being not quite right.

A picture took shape in her mind: an image of a man with a rifle crouching among the trees at the edge of the forest . . .

Then the fear came. And the bear felt it too and growled low in its throat. The girl began to move back . . .

But then she stopped.

She did not know why. Perhaps the fear was rooting her to the spot. But she did not think so. It was more a sense of the inevitable. That all she had to do was stay still for a few more seconds and it would all be over. She would not have to worry any more about who or what she was – or what she had to do.

But something else was stronger. She could feel it taking over her mind – as if she was a computer and its unknown operator had switched her to a different program.

Another image formed in her mind, not of a man this time but of a child. She did not know who it was or how it had got there but she felt it expand inside her skull until her temples were throbbing. Then, with a conscious effort of will, she hurled it away from her across the ice towards the edge of the forest.

The hunter's finger froze on the trigger. He had his target framed in the crosshairs. Distant but clear.

So why didn't he shoot?

He heard a noise surprisingly like a sob.

Even more surprisingly it seemed to be coming from him.

The image in his sights became blurred. He reached up to adjust the scope but his hand was trembling and, besides, it wasn't the sights that were blurred – it was his eyes.

He laid his head on the ground. His shoulders began to shake.

'Issat?' His companion stared at him in astonishment. The Laughing One was crying. 'What is it?'

But Issat was overwhelmed by a desperate sadness, so vast and incomprehensible he could find no words to express it.

'I saw her,' he groaned.

'Saw who?'

'My child. My little girl.'

'But Issat . . .' His friend could make no sense of this. 'You don't have a child.'

'I know,' said Issat, 'I know.' And he rolled himself into a ball and put his face in his hands and wept. And he could not explain the fear that was in his mind – and had been since he was four years old and had seen his baby sister dying in his father's arms – the fear that he too would nurse a dying child and this time it would be his own.

His companion gazed at him in growing bewilderment. Then he pressed his eye to the slit in the side of the shelter. But the wind had picked up after its brief lull and now raged with renewed vigour as if scandalized by the monstrosities it had revealed. A great cloud of snow gusted across the lake, blotting out the massive fortress and its mysterious occupants and he dropped the flap and looked down at the grieving man in fear and confusion.

'Who is she?' he said, in a voice that sounded nothing like his own. 'Why is she here?'

He would have been amazed if he had known that almost the same thoughts were running through the mind of the distant figure in red as she turned away from the fury of the wind and groped her way along the battlements toward the dark portal opened for her by her silent companion.

6

The Castle of Demons

Jade paused in the doorway, drew back a step and bobbed a little mock curtsy.

'After you,' she said to the bear.

The bear peered down the spiral stair. The steps were steep and narrow. At the first turn a feeble torch guttered in the draught from the open door. He showed his teeth in what was either an unconvincing snarl or a sheepish grin but did not move.

'Bears before girls when going down stairs,' said the girl firmly as if this was an important principle of etiquette (though, in fact, she had just made it up).

The bear looked at her again, clearly confused.

She lifted the cloak clear of the ground. The hem was wet where it had trailed in the snow.

'Dangerous,' she said. 'Might trip. Break neck.'

The bear growled but it was more of a begrudging than an angry growl and he let go of the door and placed one wary foot on the topmost step.

'Careful,' said the girl with a frown of concern.

It is not easy for a bear to descend a spiral staircase. The best way, in Jade's opinion, was to go backwards, like a toddler, lying on your stomach and putting one foot on the step below and then placing the other next to it. But possibly the bear considered this to be undignified for he always tried to go down sideways, standing more or less upright and holding on to the wall with both paws. This invariably ended in disaster.

He managed to get as far as the first turn before he lost his footing on the narrow steps. He wobbled for a moment, his claws scrabbling frantically at the stone wall and then, with a roar of anguished protest, he fell.

Jade listened to the thuds and howls until they faded into the dim interior of the castle. She shook her head sadly and with one last defiant glance over her shoulder towards the forest, lost now in the blizzard, she followed the unhappy creature cautiously down the stairs, shutting the door firmly behind her.

She found him waiting for her at the bottom, breathing heavily but apparently unhurt. She had been assured that he could feel no pain – for though he bore a striking resemblance to the European brown bear, *Ursus arctos*, he was in fact a robot, designed and manufactured in the castle laboratories.

'A fine piece of genetic engineering', according to her father, Dr Kobal. 'One of my best so far.'

Even so, it must shake up the wiring a bit, Jade thought as she followed him down the corridor.

'Poor Laurie,' she sighed. 'Just as well you've got plenty of padding, eh?'

Laurie was her pet name for the bear. It made him seem more user-friendly than a 'four hundredweight killing machine,' which was how her father described him, 'with claws that could rip out the throat of a full-grown moose with one swipe.'

Or mine with one pat, the girl thought dryly, if I get too mouthy.

He did not look like a killer to her – for all his height and weight. More like a clown: a sad, funny, furry clown, shambling down the corridor ahead of her. One of the less objectionable of her father's creations: the dark and sinister denizens of Castle Piru: the Castle of Demons.

She sensed them now, all around her, as she followed the bear down the long, gloomy corridor.

Ghostly shapes fleeing before her or peering after her from nooks and crannies when she'd gone by. You'd see a shadow on the stones at the end of the corridor, or hear a scuttling noise behind you, like the rustle of dry leaves, only to turn and find nothing was there. Sometimes, but very rarely, she'd catch a glimpse of one of the smaller creatures scuttling up the wall and disappearing through a gap in the stones. You might take it for a rat or a spider or a lizard, except that it would be a mistake to assume that anything was real in the Castle of Demons, even the rats and spiders. All was sham and illusion.

The entire building was a labyrinth and she was no nearer discovering its secrets than when she had first arrived three months ago. She suspected that if she ever tried to escape or even leave her room without an escort she would be condemned to wander the endless corridors and stairways for all eternity, never finding the way out or even the way back. With the added attraction of running into one of the horrors her father kept in the castle dungeons, but let out at night as a deterrent to burglars.

As if anyone would be foolish enough to burgle the Castle of Demons.

They had reached the corner of the corridor and

before them stretched an even longer one – far longer, surely, than the dimensions of the castle permitted. It was almost certainly a trick of the architect, aided by hidden mirrors and the smoke from the guttering torches. There was electricity in the castle but not in the corridors; only the stinking flambeaus in their iron brackets, giving off more smoke than light, aiding the illusion.

But about halfway along this corridor there was a door. Laurie stopped before it and knocked, or rather scratched on the wooden panelling with his long claws. After a moment a voice bade them enter. Laurie pushed open the door and stepped politely aside for Jade to precede him into . . . the gym.

The contrast with the gloomy, ancient corridor could hardly have been greater. The gym was lined with mirrors and wall bars and contained a vast array of equipment: rowing machines and exercise bikes and step-up machines and treadmills and weight machines of every size and description. The first impression on entering the room was that they went on for ever – like a kind of Gymnasium Hell – that hidden speakers blared out stirring martial music that Jade, from previous visits, recognized as the 'March of the Valkyries' – the dread warrior hags of the Northlands.

And hanging upside down from the wall bars in black leotard and tights, like a slim species of bat, was the chief Valkyrie herself – Barmella.

Of all the strange creatures in Castle Piru, Barmella was probably the strangest. At least to Jade.

But then, as Dr Kobal might say, they had history.

At Jade's entrance she swung her legs down over her head until her feet touched the floor and then described a series of rapid somersaults, gracefully springing off the floor on the flat of her hands and feet until she came to a stop, the right way up, directly in front of them.

'Good morning, Fraulein,' she said in her clipped German accent.

'Good morning, Fraulein,' piped Jade, as she had been instructed, struggling as usual not to look down at the floor when confronted by the searching gaze of those cold blue eyes.

Sophie Caroline Maria Baer-Mellor von Koffen was a countess, according to Dr Kobal, though the first time Jade met her she had been working as a nurse in a hospital for the criminally insane. Privately Jade called her Barmella, which was the way she pronounced her family name – Baer-Mellor. But it was also the name of a doll Jade had owned when she was a little girl in London – a strange rag doll with a large plastic head and hands.

Never pretty, the doll had not improved with age, especially when she lost an eye and her hair fell out. She also had a large dent in her forehead where Jade had thrown her against a wall in a tantrum. Jade was ashamed of this now and also of the time she had staged a funeral for her in the back garden, burying her in a cardboard shoe box in a flower bed with all her other dolls and cuddly toys as mourners. Later she had dug her up, but only to eke out a ghostly existence among the other neglected toys on the chair in Jade's bedroom.

This new Barmella also had large hands and a large head, shaved so as to appear completely bald, and although she had both eyes they gleamed with the same cold blue intensity as the single eye of the doll.

Jade could not help thinking that she *was* the doll, summoned into existence by some sinister spell of her father's to teach her a lesson about being kind to people – or at least dolls.

Certainly after a session with her in the gym Jade felt she knew how the poor doll had felt.

'You – to wait here,' said Barmella to the bear, closing the door in its face. 'You – to change zer clothes,' she said to Jade.

Jade went into the changing room and emerged a few minutes later in a pale-blue leotard with her hair tied back in a matching ribbon. She smiled cheerfully in the hope that Barmella would go easy with her. This had never worked in the past but it was worth a try. Besides, if she didn't smile things might get even worse.

'On zer bike,' snapped Barmella unnecessarily, pointing toward the row of exercise bikes lined up in front of the mirror on the far wall. Unnecessary, because Jade's exercise routine never varied. First she did ten minutes of hill climb on the bicycle, then the rowing machine, then the treadmill, then step-ups and then ten minutes on the floor mats being thrown around by Barmella and twisted into various impossible shapes – a bit like the balloons favoured by child entertainers at birthday parties.

Barmella called this Judo. Jade called it Revenge.

Jade had never been so fit in her life – but fit for what, she often wondered? It was not as if she was being trained for the Olympics. Jade's talents were all in the mind. She could read people's thoughts. She could divine their deepest, innermost fears and even, on occasion, make them real. Or at least, *appear* real.

It didn't work with everyone – not with her father, for instance, or Barmella – and it gave her terrible migraines. But it was a skill well worth having. A power that could give her power over others. Or so her father had told her. Jade was not sure she wanted power over others but she agreed that it could be useful at times. Her father had promised to help her get better at it – and master it so it didn't give her a headache. But so far he had done nothing.

She wondered sometimes – most of the time in fact – why he had bothered to bring her here at all.

But for the best part of an hour Jade could think of little besides survival. Barmella was a fanatical trainer. And through every exercise she kept up a flow of instruction in the screeching voice of a drill sergeant. By the time they reached the floor mats Jade was exhausted in mind and body. She was incapable of remembering the holds and movements that Barmella had taught her, let alone executing them. She just let Barmella throw her around like, well, like a rag doll.

She tottered off to the changing room more dead than alive. But after her shower she felt wonderfully refreshed – and ravenously hungry.

Laurie was waiting for her outside the door, exactly where he had been when Barmella closed it in his face. His eyes looked dull, as if something had been switched off in his brain – probably to save the batteries. But thin wisps of frozen breath emerged from his mouth and as soon as Jade appeared a small light appeared in his eyes and he turned with a brief grunt and shambled off down the corridor.

At the end of the corridor was another door. A quite ordinary door except that it was guarded by two stuffed flamingos, wearing bearskins. Rather like the guards at Buckingham Palace, only thinner and pinker. Although they were clearly dead and their pink feathers looked decidedly the worse for wear, the head of the nearest swivelled round at their approach and one of its black eyes seemed to regard them with an inner glow from beneath the bushy brim of the bearskin. This did not surprise Jade in the least. Every movement in the castle was recorded by hidden cameras – usually concealed in stuffed animals or birds or suits of armour.

As Jade passed she breathed on the lens, shrouding it in a cloud of frozen breath. A futile gesture but one that gave her some small satisfaction – and the stuffed flamingo none at all.

Laurie scratched on the door and after a moment it swung open. Jade shielded her eyes against the sudden glare of sunlight as she stepped into the room within.

It was like stepping from the Arctic Circle into a tropical rainforest.

As her eyes adjusted to the glare she saw humming birds on whirring wings and a flight of parakeets darting through the foliage high above her head. Her ears were filled with the sound of running water and birdsong. Palm trees and ornamental figs jostled with bamboo and giant fern, citrus trees, banana and pomegranate with gorgeous red flowers; flowers everywhere, in great terracotta pots on the floor or winding among the trees: bright orange and pink hibiscus, lobster-claw heliconias, orchids and begonias, others she could not name. And a waterfall, tumbling down from a rock wall into a sparkling pool.

The Sun Terrace.

As this was the far north of Lapland in the dead of winter, it was not real sun, of course; it was an illusion, created by UV lights high in the ceiling, hidden by the forest canopy. But it was one of the more pleasant aspects of life in Castle Piru . . .

And beside the pool, having breakfast at a small table, sat its creator.

Jade's father, Dr Kobal.

7

Kobal

Jade took off her cloak and hung it on the hornbill standing by the door, put on a pair of sunglasses and walked through the jungle to join the dark figure by the pool, wondering what kind of mood he would be in today and what problems it would cause her.

You could usually tell his mood from what he was wearing, but not always. He had a vast wardrobe of different costumes, many of them as exotic and colourful as the plants were, but you never knew if he was wearing them because they genuinely appealed to him or because it was part of some elaborate hoax: a wonderful joke he was playing on the rest of the world for his own private amusement.

Today he was dressed as a monk – a black monk.

Usually this meant he wanted a bit of privacy, especially if he wore the cowl up so you couldn't see his face. Sometimes he would prowl around in it at night, and if you ran into him in the castle corridors or on the battlements he'd drift past you without a word and you were not supposed to speak to him, so you could never be certain if it was him or someone else – some *thing* he'd made in his laboratory and allowed out for a stroll. But this morning the cowl was thrown back over his shoulders and his long hair was tied in a ponytail; he wore a pair of designer sunglasses studded with small diamonds and, instead of a cross, a small silver star on a chain around his neck. And on his feet, instead of the humble sandals you might expect of a monk, he wore a pair of gold lamé flip-flops.

'Morning,' said Jade, restraining herself from remarking on the flip-flops or pointing out that he still had the price tag – one hundred and fifty-five euros – stuck to the rubber sole. She had no doubt at all that it was deliberate. Another piece of theatre.

He looked up from his newspaper.

'You look a little flushed this morning,' he remarked archly. 'Been for a stroll?'

'I've been to the gym,' said Jade in surprise.

She went to the gym most mornings. It was in her timetable.

'And before that?'

'Oh.' Jade flushed a bit more. 'I went out on the battlements,' she said, reaching for the jug of orange juice.

'You don't say? Something the matter with the courtyard?'

'I wanted to look out over the lake.'

'Oh really? And what did you see?'

'Nothing much,' she said, managing to avoid his eye. She could feel it on her, though, weighing her up.

'I guess the real question should be, who saw *you*?'

She contrived a careless shrug. 'Who do you think is out there?' she asked him.

'I know very well who is out there,' he replied coldly. 'Impudent miss. But until now I did not realize how close they were to the castle walls. It's very foolish of them. I might have to send one of our friends to point this out.'

Jade glanced at him sharply.

By 'friends' he presumably meant one of the creatures in the basement. She shuddered. He was really quite angry, she realized.

'And it's very foolish of you,' he went on, 'to

venture out on to the battlements when I've given you very clear warnings of the danger you're in. There are people out there who are trying to kill you, do you understand that?'

'Yes,' she said, trying to sound defiant but feeling quite small all of a sudden.

It distressed her that people were trying to kill her.

People who thought she was some kind of a freak or monster.

'So please don't do it again,' he said, 'unless you have my express permission.'

Right on, Doc, she said. But not aloud. Instead she laid a postcard on the table between them. It was one of a series he had given her – to let her family know she was all right. It showed the Taj Mahal in India and it would be posted from somewhere else in the world. On the other side she had written: '*Safe and well. Hope all well with you. Don't worry about me. Saw Safina beat Jakovic in the Australian Open.*'

She was not allowed to go into more detail than that but Kobal said that each time she wrote she should include some news item so they would know it was a recent message. What he didn't know was that in each message she made one deliberate spelling mistake. In this one, for instance, *Jakovic* should have been spelled *Jankovic*. Jade was crazy about tennis and her Aunt Em, at least, would know she would never get the spellings wrong. Jade hoped that she would realise the missing 'n' was significant. In fact it was a clue to where she was. If whoever was reading them put all the missing letters together from the last six cards they would spell *Finlan* . . .

Always assuming they had been sent.

Kobal glanced briefly at the postcard and then returned to his newspaper. *The Washington Post.* Today's edition. Even though it was probably only three in the morning, Washington time. He must have printed it from the Internet in his study. He could have read it straight off the computer, of course, but he was old-fashioned in many ways. He always liked a newspaper with his breakfast. Usually an American newspaper. He spoke with a faint American accent, at least some of the time, and insisted that his home town was New York City. But Jade had an idea he had been born somewhere else, possibly somewhere in the Middle East, like Lebanon. Somewhere warm and sunny, anyway. Which was why, whenever he was obliged to live in a northern climate, even north of the Arctic Circle, he always had a hothouse built into the design.

He reached out a hand for his coffee. It was in a mug with a picture of Mother Theresa on it. Jade stuck her tongue out at him, secure in the knowledge that he could not see through a newspaper.

Though you could never be sure.

She still could not believe he was her father. He looked far too young for a start. He said it was in the genes but she wasn't convinced. And they didn't look at all alike. He was dark and she was fair. He had long black hair and hers was short and tawny blonde. She had greenish-blue eyes and a snub nose. His eyes were brown, almost black, and his nose long and sharp, like a hawk's. She could never imagine calling him Daddy or Dad. He had told her to call him Father but most of the time she thought of him as Kobal – a mysterious stranger, not to be trusted.

'I told you – I'm older than I look,' he said, still not taking his eyes from the newspaper. 'And you take after your mother – at least in appearance.'

Jade was startled, though she was well aware of his ability to read her thoughts whenever he chose. She normally tried to keep her mind blank when she was with him but it wasn't easy and he sometimes took her by surprise.

'Excuse me?' she said to give herself time to think.

This time he put down the newspaper and looked at her.

'Do I look like the kind of man who would lie to his own daughter?' he demanded.

The simple answer to this was yes.

Instead Jade said, 'But if you're *not* my father you wouldn't be, would you?'

He appeared puzzled. 'Wouldn't be what?'

'Lying to your own daughter.'

She couldn't stop herself from smiling angelically.

He gazed at her for a moment in silence. Then he said, 'Has anyone every told you that no one likes a smartypants?'

They had, frequently. In her former life. But there was something else on her mind now.

'So who *was* my mother?' she demanded. 'My *real* mother.'

It wasn't the first time she had asked this but it was the first time he had ever mentioned her mother without prompting and she thought he might be in the mood to tell her more.

She was wrong.

'Not the time or place,' he said and disappeared behind his newspaper again.

Jade glowered at him but decided not to pursue

the matter further, at least for the time being. She crossed over to the long table where breakfast was laid out. A lot of breakfast. Cereals of every description and great bowls of fruit in iced bowls, baskets of warm rolls and many different kinds of bread, jars of jam and marmalade, soft white cheeses and yoghurt, sliced ham and figs . . . and a row of stainless-steel dishes on a hotplate containing food more suited to the climate outside: porridge, bacon and eggs, sausages and mushrooms, baked beans, tomatoes, hash browns and fried bread. Jade had no idea who prepared all this. She wouldn't have been surprised to know it was Laurie or one of his furry friends. She'd once found a long brown hair in her porridge.

She looked round and saw him standing next to a tree, slyly scratching his bottom up and down on it as if he had fleas. (Do robot bears have fleas? she wondered.) He kept well in the background while Kobal was around.

She loaded up a tray and carried it back to the table.

Just as she sat down a fruit bat swooped low over their heads and dumped on her before performing a neat aerial manoeuvre to land in one of the trees, hanging upside down and swaying slightly, like a large black fig.

Jade tutted loudly. 'Can't you do something about that?' she complained as she mopped up the mess with a napkin.

'It's a fruit bat,' Kobal said from behind his newspaper. 'It eats fruit, it excretes fruit. You don't want to be interfering with nature.'

But then he looked up at it thoughtfully.

'No,' she said firmly.

He went back to his newspaper.

She started breakfast. But after a few moments an idea occurred to her. She balanced a prune on her spoon, took careful aim and hurled it with a powerful flick of the wrist at the fruit bat. She missed but not by much. She reckoned it would get the message.

If Kobal noticed, he pretended not to. Jade felt unaccountably irritated.

'It's been snowing for three days now,' she remarked.

No response.

'Probably all night, too,' she continued. 'Not that you can tell the difference between night and day, of course, in this place.'

He turned a page. Jade sighed. One of the more

inconvenient aspects of being kidnapped, she reflected as she inspected her porridge for bear hairs, is that you cannot phone your friends when you feel like it, or text them, or even send them emails. There were other minor irritants – like fruit bats dumping on you – but it was the sense of total isolation that really freaked her. Especially on the dark days when there was a full-scale blizzard raging outside and the wind was shrieking around the castle walls and all you could see if you looked out of the windows was a frenzy of swirling snow.

'Doesn't it ever stop?' she demanded querulously.

Kobal lowered the newspaper and looked at her.

'Doesn't what ever stop?'

'The snow.'

He looked one way and then the other with exaggerated attention. Then he looked up into the air.

'It's not snowing here,' he observed.

A white cockatoo skimmed down from one of the trees and landed on his shoulder. At least, it looked like a cockatoo but it was probably something he'd made earlier. He fed it a piece of fruit from his plate. Jade observed it with distaste. She didn't like the way it held the fig in its claws or its horrible black tongue or the way it looked at her as it ate. There was something faintly reptilian about it. Like it would just as soon be eating her.

'I mean outside,' she said. She threw her arms in the air as if making a small explosion. The cockatoo took off in alarm.

'Look at it.' She pointed towards the long narrow windows of the Sun Terrace, not much wider than arrow slits. But the glass was misted over and there was nothing to see, except that it was snowing. 'It's always snowing and it's always windy and it's always night.'

Kobal laid his newspaper down with a sigh and topped up his Mother Theresa mug with fresh coffee.

'You live in Lapland, you gotta put up with a certain amount of snow,' he pointed out, as if she'd had any choice in the matter of where she did or didn't live. 'And wind,' he added, after a moment's reflection. 'And night.'

'Well . . . paint me red and call me Santa,' said Jade with a fair attempt at his accent.

He observed her with his head on one side and a dangerous look in his eye.

'Someone get out of the wrong side of bed this morning?'

But she knew she'd got him niggled. He always

had to rise to a challenge. She could see him thinking about it as he spread cloudberry jam on his toast.

'We could go somewhere warm,' he said.

'Somewhere warm?' she repeated cautiously, though she could not prevent her hopes from rising. 'Oh yeah? How?'

'We could fly.'

'You crashed the aeroplane,' she reminded him.

He brooded on this for a moment. It was not true that he personally had crashed the aeroplane but he had been in it at the time. So had Jade. They had crashlanded on a frozen lake in the forest during their flight from England and been forced to continue on foot and on a reindeer sled Kobal had stolen. It was three months ago now but she still shuddered to think of it. Being in a plane crash tends to stick in the memory. The reindeer sled had been a bit of a trial too.

'We could go on a motorbike,' he said thoughtfully. 'A motorbike and sidecar.'

Jade was inclined to point out that the far north of Lapland in winter is not ideal for travelling on a motorbike – even with a sidecar – but he might take this as another challenge. Instead she suggested: 'Why not a motor *car*? Or a snowcat. At least for the first thousand miles or so.'

Kobal frowned while he picked cloudberry seeds from his teeth.

'We *could*,' he said thoughtfully, 'but it's nothing like as cool.' She wondered if this was his idea of a joke. 'And I could wear my long leather German Army coat,' he continued, 'and my Russian motorcyclist's leather cap with the demister goggles.' He stood up, throwing his napkin on the table. 'Come on,' he said. 'Let's do it.'

Oh no, she thought, what have I done?

'Now?'

'Now,' he said firmly. 'Before you get even more bored.'

Jade winced. It was always dangerous to suggest to Kobal that you might be a bit bored. He had all kinds of ways of making life more interesting for you – and they were never pleasant.

She inclined her head towards the windows. 'What about *Them*. Out there. The people who are trying to kill me.'

'Oh, we don't have to worry about *Them*,' he said carelessly, 'not with this particular beast.'

Jade didn't like the sound of this, or the way he was looking at her.

He led her along the side of the pool and stopped

beside the waterfall She watched, mystified, as he reached behind one of the ferns and tugged at something in the rock wall.

After a moment the water slowed to a trickle and a section of rock slid aside to reveal a small, square, windowless room.

'After you,' said Kobal with a smile.

8

The Killers in the Basement

The doors slid smoothly shut – but not before Kobal
had glided through the narrowing gap to join her.
She tried to hide her relief.

'Only teasing,' he said. He was wearing his
teasing smile, the one that made her want to punch
him. He reached toward a brass panel on the wall.
'Going down,' he said in a mock English accent and
she gasped as the floor moved beneath her feet. Then
she realized.

A lift.

She had not known there was a lift in Castle Piru.
It was just like Kobal to keep it to himself and let
everyone else struggle up and down the spiral stairs.
But where was he taking her?

A light flickered above their heads.

'First floor. Haberdashery, toiletries, cosmetics, separates and ladies' lingerie,' he sang out as if he was a lift-operator in an old-fashioned department store.

Then – in what she thought of as his camp New Yorker voice – he added, 'I'm just crazy about shopping, aren't you? Especially in a place with *style*. Tradition. Good service. "Are you being served?" Did you go shopping much in London? I expect your Aunt Em took you for tea at Harrods; she used to like that sort of thing – when I knew her, anyway. Harrods, Selfridges, Liberty's, John Lewis . . . Personally I prefer Paris. The Galeries Lafayette in the Boulevard Haussmann. A food hall to die for. And Bon Marché – the oldest department store in the world, did you know that?'

He was trying to distract her – and it almost worked. Especially at the mention of her Aunt Em. She remembered the outings they used to have when she was little: the zoo in Regent's Park and Madame Tussaud's and the Horse Guards in the Mall and the Christmas grotto at Selfridges . . .

Another light in the panel above the door. The ground floor. And they were still going down. Her heart sank with the lift.

She had never been below ground level at Castle Piru. But she knew there was at least one floor below that. She had seen the stairs going down and guessed they led to the old dungeons where Kobal did his experiments and kept the ones that had gone wrong, or were too dangerous to let out. Once while she was in the small courtyard she had heard strange noises from below ground – a throb of engines and a kind of choking noise that was something between a howl and a laugh and a creaking gate. It wasn't wise to dwell on the nightmares Kobal kept down there . . . and you didn't want to get any closer to them.

The lift stopped.

'Lower ground,' he chanted. 'Hardware, kitchenware, electrical goods, garden furniture and –' with a smile she didn't at all trust '– Santa's grotto.'

She looked at him sharply but then the doors slid open and he gave her an ironic bow and said, 'After you.'

And she stepped out of the lift into . . . a garage.

A garage or an underground car park. Dimly lit and smelling of oil and petrol and rubber tyres. Most of the vehicles were quite old and some rather the worse for wear. There were several vintage sports cars, an ancient Rolls Royce – Jade recognized it from the radiator grille − a couple of large black American saloons, like old-fashioned gangster cars, and several military vehicles − from the Second World War by the look of them, some with the Nazi swastika on the side. There was even a tank − a little tank with a red star on the gun turret. The whole place was like a museum. And decidedly spooky, like a room full of ghosts . . .

Then she looked up and saw the balloon. A giant brown balloon shaped like a fat cigar, with a kind of cabin slung underneath with a propeller at the back, as if it was a ship.

'That's my Zeppelin,' said Kobal, from behind her. 'The original prototype made by Graf von Zeppelin in 1898. The model for the ones the Germans used to bomb London in World War One, though they were much bigger of course.'

'Of course,' she said faintly, not having the faintest idea what he was talking about.

'Whole fleets of them bombing London,' Kobal mused in a dreamy voice, as if he wished he'd had the idea himself. 'The first true flying machines. Then along came the fixed-wing aircraft and consigned them to oblivion. Pity really.'

He walked on and stopped beside a motorbike and

sidecar parked in the shadow of the tank. It was painted a dingy brown colour like all the other military vehicles but although it was an old design it looked brand new. Or at least newly renovated. The chrome sparkled even in the dim light, the working parts positively gleamed with oil and grease and the tyres looked like they'd never been on a road.

'What do you think?' said Kobal.

Jade shrugged. She was more interested in why he had brought her here. Were they really going on a trip?

She wouldn't put it past him.

But all she had on was a thin sweater and a pair of jeans and trainers. She'd even left her cloak behind in the Sun Terrace. And he was still in his monk's robe with his gold lamé sandals. Hardly the thing for tearing round the Arctic Circle in winter. Unless you were totally bonkers – which, of course, he was.

'Take a look around,' he invited her with a casual wave of his hand. 'Be back in a minute – but don't touch anything.'

Then he was gone – through a small door marked *Staff Only*.

What staff? She peered around her, even into the darker corners. No, she was quite alone. But she still felt as if she was being watched. Hidden cameras probably, like everywhere else. But it felt as if the vehicles themselves were watching her.

She shook her head at the notion.

And yet there was definitely something odd about them. Something sinister. As if . . .

As if something terrible had happened down here and the silent vehicles had been witness to it.

Then she knew.

Terrible things *had* happened. Not here, but in the vehicles themselves before they had come here.

They were killers. All of them. She could sense it, with a dreadful certainty. They had killed the people who drove them or the people who travelled in them – or the people who got in their way. She could almost hear the screams in the moment before they died and smell the sharp, acrid smell of overheated engines and burning rubber and sometimes burning flesh.

But why would Kobal do that? Why would he bring them here?

No. She was being fanciful, letting her imagination get the better of her. That was the trouble with having a mind like hers. You never knew what was real and what was imagined.

She took a deep breath and walked up to the motorbike.

It seemed quite ordinary, except for being so old-fashioned. There was a single leather bucket seat in the sidecar. It looked quite comfortable, almost cosy.

'Get in. Try it for size.'

She turned and beheld a vision in long leather coat and boots and a tight-fitting leather helmet with goggles. He hadn't been joking.

So was he serious about going somewhere?

Then she saw the other helmet under his arm. A space-age helmet painted black with a black Perspex visor.

'No,' she cried.

'Get in the sidecar,' he said. Almost tiredly, as if to a wayward child.

He opened the door and she climbed in like a zombie and sank down into the leather seat. The blood had drained from her face and all her strength with it and she felt as if she was going to be sick.

'It's only a game,' he said, as he fitted the helmet over her head.

9

The Mind Game

Jade moved her head from side to side but she could see nothing through the Perspex visor. It was like wearing a blindfold. The helmet was not particularly heavy but it felt strange, as if someone had laid both hands on her head and was pressing gently down – and there was a faint tingling sensation on the surface of her skull as if she'd just brushed her hair and it was tingling with electricity.

But she had worn the helmet once before and she knew it was the electrodes pressing on the power points of her brain.

Dimly, she sensed someone climbing on to the motorbike and then a voice she vaguely recognized as Kobal's.

'Ready?'

As if. But what could she do?

'Ready,' she said, trying to sound confident. Or defiant. *Scare me if you can . . .*

She felt like she was at the dentist's and he was about to drill right into her brain, which in a way he was.

But why the motorbike?

There was a sudden noise from the kick-starter, once, twice and then a roar as he opened the throttle. *Vroom, vroom.*

And then a light. A powerful beam of light from the motorcycle headlamp. She twisted her head to the side but she couldn't see him even though she knew he was sitting right beside her. All she could see was the beam of light piercing the darkness.

And bouncing off the wall directly in front of them.

'Then let's do it,' said the voice.

And then they were moving. Fast.

Hurtling down the beam of light . . . straight at the wall . . .

Jade opened her mouth to scream but no sound came; she tried to jump but she couldn't move. It was like being in a dream and you knew you had to wake up but you couldn't. And you tried to run but you couldn't. And the wall seemed to be rushing her out of the darkness, like her own death racing to meet her . . .

She raised both arms above her head and—

It wasn't a wall any more – it was a forest.

They were driving along a long, straight road through a forest. Snow-covered firs seemed to hurtle past on either side. She looked up and saw the treetops outlined against the night sky and the snow drifting gently down.

But it wasn't falling on the motorbike or on the road.

Part of her brain was rationalizing all this and thinking: *This is not real, I am not here.* It was coming from her head – or being fed into her head by the helmet. And the motorbike was just a prop. A way of making it *seem* real. Or just another mad idea of Kobal's so it would seem like they were travelling together. Father and child. Teacher and pupil.

But in reality they were going nowhere. It was a game, a very sophisticated computer game, but instead of watching it unfold on a screen, it was as if the game was in her head. *Or her head was in the game.*

There were many games in Castle Piru but this

was *the* game and it terrified her. She felt as if she was in a dream that she couldn't control and in which terrible things might happen, things that would freeze your blood and make you scream and scream until you went stark, staring mad. But unlike an ordinary dream, you couldn't wake up if it got out of hand, even if it looked like you were going to die.

She felt the panic, then, and she forced herself to concentrate, to fight it.

Be cool.

She had only played the game once before and then it hadn't been on a motorbike. The motorbike made it more difficult. Or rather the sidecar did. Because she was just a passenger. Kobal was in the driving seat.

Somehow, she knew he could see everything that she could see. They were *her* thoughts but he was reading them and almost certainly guiding them in a certain direction.

Last time she had played the game she had lost control very quickly. She would arrive some place – a forest in England, a circus in India, a monastery in China or Tibet – but then the images would drift away from her and she would lose them. She would start to think about something else – like shopping with her Aunt Em or going to a museum.

Kobal had found this irritating.

She had the feeling that now, when she arrived somewhere – somewhere he wanted to be – he would take control from her. Or he would force her to stick in there, to see it through to the end.

It had stopped snowing. And the trees were changing. They were no longer firs. They were more like the trees you found in England. Oak or beech or something – she was no expert. And it wasn't night any more. It wasn't sunny. Just kind of grey. A grey, drab light, with perhaps a hint of ground fog. Like a wood at dawn.

Not that she'd ever been in a wood at dawn.

But she had an idea that she knew it – and that it was the Royal Forest of Windsor, where she had been born.

They were slowing down. And then they were in a clearing. And she knew this, too. She had been here before, the last time . . .

A clearing in the forest, where three tracks meet.

One was the track she had just emerged from. Except that when she looked back it didn't look the same. It wasn't surfaced and it wasn't straight. It was a rough earthen track winding through the forest.

Then she realized she was no longer in the sidecar. The motorbike had disappeared – and Kobal with it. She was on her own.

But not quite. There was a figure standing about halfway down one of the tracks, half hidden by the mist and the shadows of the trees so that it appeared to be floating. The figure of a monk in a long black robe with a cowl over his head.

Kobal?

He lifted an arm and beckoned. Then turned and walked away.

Jade stayed where she was.

After a few steps, the monk looked back over his shoulder and beckoned again – more insistently now.

What should she do?

She wasn't sure.

She looked down the path to her right . . . and there was an identical figure, making the same signal.

One of them had to be Kobal – but which one? It was impossible to tell with the cowls covering their faces . . .

She looked down the third path, expecting to see another monk. But there was no one. Then – a movement, as if someone was hiding behind a tree – a glimpse of red . . .

'Mummy?'

She heard herself saying the word aloud – or at least someone said it, in a scared little-girl voice. A meaningless word now, for she did not know who her mother was. Not her *real* mother.

And then she thought of another possibility.

'Aunt Em?'

Her godmother. Or at least the woman who had claimed to be her godmother, the woman Jade had *believed* to be godmother until three months ago when she had stopped believing in anyone any more.

But why would her godmother be hiding behind a tree in a forest?

Except that she had always hidden from her, in a sense. She had certainly hidden the truth from her.

'Aunt Em?'

No sound, no movement. The forest silent, waiting . . . The path leading on into the distance, a distant, greenish haze . . .

And then the figure stepped out from behind the tree. It was wearing a red coat – in a shiny material like a raincoat – with a hood and black boots. But it was walking away from her down the path.

It did not beckon her, as the monks had. But Jade knew she was expected to follow.

She hesitated for a moment.

Who to trust? The monks – or the woman in red? She was sure it was a woman. Aunt Em – or someone else?

She didn't trust any of them. Why should she? She only trusted herself – and then not very often, not with any confidence.

The figure was still walking up the path, without a backward glance. Soon she would be out of sight.

Little Red Riding Hood, thought Jade scornfully. And the scorn made her reckless.

She began to follow her down the track.

And instantly it divided again. Not once, not three times – but as if it had burst in every direction, like an explosion. A starburst.

She was in a blaze of light, a blaze of brilliant white light that forced her to shield her eyes against the glare . . . She could no longer see the figure in red but she could see a number of new paths leading off, seemingly in every direction, like blades of light – or the points of a star.

She stood, paralysed by fear and indecision, blinded by the light . . . She felt that she could not stay where she was or she would be lost, her identity burned up in the star. She hurled herself forward, shielding her face with her arms, running directly down one of the beams of light . . .

And then it began to change. It was still bright but not so painful, not so white. More like . . . sunshine. As if she had just stepped outside from a dark room and her eyes were still adjusting to it. She stood still and squinted into the glare . . . and slowly she began to make out shapes and colours, indistinct at first and puzzling. A brilliant blue sky with birds circling at a great height. And hills, rising all around. Small hills, more like . . . sand dunes.

But they were not made of sand.

They were made of rubbish.

Great mounds of rubbish. Waste paper and plastic bags, bottles and tin cans, rags and rotting food . . . all manner of refuse twenty or thirty metres high, as tall as a house, with a great cloud of flies and other insects buzzing and crawling all over them.

And the smell . . . She could smell it as if she was really there. An overwhelming stench of decay – and the acrid reek of burning rubbish.

And then she saw the children.

A small army of children playing in the filth.

Except that they were not playing.

They were searching through it. Searching very

determinedly, with serious faces. Small brown children dressed in rags, very much like the rubbish itself. And they had black plastic bags tied around their waists for collecting things. Plastic bottles, bits of glass and clothing . . . anything that caught their eye.

And two of them were eating a pizza.

Jade screwed her face up in disgust for it was clearly a pizza they had found in the rubbish, still in its white delivery box, and they were sharing it between them and picking bits off it and eating them.

She almost cried out to them – to tell them to stop it. That it was dirty, disgusting . . . And then a shadow passed over her and a large bird dropped out of the sky and landed awkwardly between her and the two boys.

The ugliest, most revolting bird she had ever seen.

A vulture.

But bigger and uglier than any vulture she had seen in wildlife films. Its plumage was black and grey and its head red and yellow with a long scrawny neck and a wrinkly red sack – its *crop*, Jade remembered this was called – where it digested its food.

It was after the pizza but the children weren't going to give it up so easily. They were yelling at it in a language Jade could not understand and it was screaming back at them, screaming and flapping its wings as it hopped about among the rubbish, stretching out its red-and-yellow beak and its scrawny neck. One of the children, the bigger of the two, had a stick and he was striking at it but not getting close enough to hit it. Then another bird dropped down . . . and another.

And then the earth began to move.

Jade felt it tremble beneath her feet and she thought it was an earthquake.

But it was the rubbish moving.

The whole tip was sliding – and Jade and the two children and the three vultures were directly in its path.

The birds took off with shrieks of alarm and the children started to run. But their feet were sinking into the rubbish, as if the ground was opening up from under them . . .

And then they were gone and the dust rose around them like a great black cloud blotting the sun.

Jade had just stood there, rooted to the spot, too shocked to run or shout or do anything. But miraculously the avalanche of filth stopped almost at her feet. She stood there for a moment in the acrid cloud of dust, coughing, almost blinded – and then she started to run. But not away. She moved without thinking, scrambling up the slope of foetid, stinking rubbish on her hands and knees, sobbing and shouting for help – though she did not know who could hear her or who could give it. When she reached the spot where she had last seen the children she began to dig into it with her bare hands, hurling it away from her with frantic haste until a hole opened at her feet: a cone-shaped pit growing deeper and deeper . . . And then she was sliding down it and she could see one of the children below and she went after him like a terrier after a rabbit . . . down, down into the tunnel of filth until the light faded and the darkness closed around her.

10

The Watchers

The two men were having breakfast. Cold sausage with rye bread and beer. It was three days since their last hot meal.

'Pancakes,' said Issat longingly, raising his hand to chin height. 'Stacked this high and melting with honey.'

'With whipped cream and berries,' said Biera, who was the younger of the two.

'Cinnamon and sugar.'

'And coffee. All the cups you can drink. Hot, black and strong.'

'Soon,' said Issat with a sigh. Today was meant to be their last day in the hide. They were due to be relieved before noon by two of the herdsmen from their village. If they could get through in the blizzard.

They ate in silence, lost in their thoughts, while the wind howled around their puny shelter and the snow piled up even higher on the roof.

Then Issat frowned and cocked his head. 'D'you hear that?' he said.

'What?' Biera listened for a moment. Then he said: 'It's just the wind.'

But Issat was still frowning and shaking his head.

'No, it's . . . more of a kind of a . . . of a snuffling sound,' he said.

He squirmed round on to his stomach and peered through the slit in the side of the shelter. But he could see nothing. Nothing but snow, billowing across the wide expanse of the frozen lake. The castle had vanished behind a veil of snow and darkness.

Then he heard it again. It *could* be the wind but it was more like someone breathing. Or a pig grunting. And very close to the hide.

He took the rifle out of its waterproof cover and jerked a cartridge into the breech.

'What would be out in this?' Biera grumbled. 'Even the wolves have more sense.'

But there was fear in his voice.

The forest was full of large predators, even in the worst of weather. The bears could be counted on to hibernate – normal bears, at any rate, the ones that didn't live in castles – but not the lynx nor the wolverine nor the wolf. And there were rumours of other creatures, besides. Creatures that had only recently appeared in the forest and that no one could put a name to.

Some said they were mutants caused by radiation blown across Russia from the nuclear reactor at Chernobyl. Monstrous freaks of nature that were the stuff of nightmares. Others said they were bred specially in the Castle of Demons and released into the forest to scare the locals into keeping their distance.

But why? What could be happening there that was so secret?

Experiments, the old ones said, shaking their heads. The Russians up to their old tricks. They blamed the Russians for everything. Even climate change. They had plenty of cause, they said, in the past.

Last November two herders had gone missing while they were rounding up reindeer on the shores of Lake Piru. The police had been called in of course but these were the Badlands on the border between Russia and Finland and the investigation came to nothing.

There had been a meeting in the village about it

and they had decided to do something about it themselves. As was the way of the *Sami*. Their shaman, Jussa Proksi, had told them they must keep a watch on the castle through the winter to report on all the comings and goings. But he had said nothing about shooting anyone. Just watch, he said, and tell me everything you see. Only shoot if it's in self-defence.

But you couldn't tell Issat anything. He had always been a bit wild. Always boasting about his training as a sniper in the Finnish Defence Force. He was the most dangerous predator in the forest, he said.

He fumbled with the bindings on the flap that covered the entrance to the hide until suddenly the wind caught it and whipped it back with a flurry of snow. Biera shivered and huddled deeper into his survival suit. Issat lowered his goggles over his eyes, pushed the rifle ahead of him through the flap and wriggled out into the storm.

'Just shout if you need any help,' muttered Biera sourly, pulling the flap shut after him and holding it against the wind.

Issat stood up and looked about him. Nothing. Nothing he could see anyway. The snow felt like gravel hurled into his face. He wiped at his goggles with a gloved hand but it didn't help much. He stumbled round the shelter, floundering through a metre of snow. Biera was right. What creature, man, beast or mutant, would venture out in this?

He stood for a moment, listening. The wind howled through the trees and across the lake. There was nothing here.

He might as well take a leak, though, now he was outside the hide. He leaned his rifle against a tree and fumbled with his zip. Then he looked up into the tree . . .

Biera heard the scream from inside the hide.

'Issat!' he called.

No response.

'Issat? If you're kidding me . . .'

Not a sound.

Except . . . He leaned his ears against the side of the shelter. There *was* something. A kind of . . . grunting, tearing noise.

Hastily now he took his own gun from its cover. An ordinary hunter's rifle, a Sako, but powerful enough to bring down a full-grown elk.

'Issat,' he called. 'I'm coming out.'

He didn't want Issat shooting at him by mistake.

He scrambled swiftly through the gap and stood

up, bracing himself against the storm and holding his rifle close to his chest. At the edge of the lake a bulky figure was bending over something lying in the snow.

'Issat?' he called uncertainly . . .

The figure turned.

But it wasn't Issat.

Issat was lying in the snow. What was left of him. This was something else.

A glimpse – no more – of a face . . . if it *was* a face. A long muzzle. Yellow eyes in a mask of hair, matted with blood. Lips drawn back to show a mouthful of teeth or fangs.

If he had been asked to describe it, Biera would have said it was a cross between a bear and a baboon.

But no one was asking. And he would never tell.

It bounded towards him and he saw now it was more ape than bear.

He fired one shot. He could not have missed at such a range. But for all the difference it made he might as well have thrown a snowball.

The first blow sent the gun flying from his hands. The second smashed his jaw. The third would have laid him unconscious, if he hadn't passed out already.

And then the fangs were at his throat.

11

The Lost Children

She was drowning in rubbish. If this was a dream, now was the time to wake up: to snap out of the nightmare and find herself in her own bed, fighting with the bedclothes and yelling blue murder . . .

But she did not wake up. There was no bed, no bedclothes, and she was fighting with filth. Tons and tons of it, above and below and all around her. Plastic bottles and bags, old newspapers and tin cans, rags and bones, common and garden refuse and the sweepings of the streets, food packaging and food itself, rotten and crawling – the waste of an entire neighbourhood.

She fought it like a swimmer fights the sea, kicking with her feet and thrashing with her arms. But you couldn't swim in it and you couldn't walk in it. It gave way beneath her and it collapsed on top of her. And only one of her hands was free; the other hung on to the boy. He was somewhere beneath her, dragging her down with him. But she refused to let him go. She hung on to him as if her own life depended on it, though it seemed likely they would both die.

And then the rubbish stopped moving. Or she stopped sinking into it. As if she had touched bottom. She could breathe – just about – but it was dark and there was a great weight pressing down on her. It was hard not to panic. She tried to push the rubbish away with her free hand but she couldn't move it. It felt like being gripped in a vice. Something sharp was digging into her shoulder. She squirmed about to try and get away from it and the rubbish started to slide again. But this time she didn't slide with it. She hung suspended at an angle of about forty-five degrees. And there was light. Not much but enough to see her hand in front of her face. She pushed again and this time she could move her arm and a small hole appeared above her – a tunnel of light. She clawed at it, making it wider. It was sunlight – of sorts. A hazy, dingy sunlight, as if filtered through mist or dust. She kicked her feet like a swimmer and though she was not rising the rubbish was sinking. The tide of filth was receding.

She knew she was not asleep but it was, in a sense, a bit like waking from a nightmare. For she was lying on a mattress. A filthy old mattress, leaking horsehair with bits of spring sticking out of it – and into her. But it had surely saved her life. A life raft in a sea of rubbish.

Except that she was not quite out of it yet. She was lying on her side and her right arm was still buried up to the shoulder and she could feel something pulling her down.

The boy!

She still had hold of him – or he had hold of her.

She tugged and heaved with her right arm and dug frantically around with her left, scooping away at the rubbish and hurling it back over her shoulder – and suddenly he came rising up out of it like a startled rabbit. A boy of about her own age, maybe a little younger, certainly smaller. A very dirty boy but very much alive.

She helped him climb up on to the mattress with her, their life raft, and they gazed about them. Rubbish, rubbish everywhere, as far as the eye could see and the sun a dirty yellow orb floating high above them in the mist.

Not mist – dust.

She began to cough and then to retch. Her sense of smell had returned and the stench was revolting.

The boy was saying something to her but she couldn't understand him.

'Do you speak English?' she asked him. Her voice was a croak, not like her own voice at all, but it must have been because he was staring at her, as if she was a ghost.

'My name's Jade,' she said. 'I'm from Finland.'

Then she realized how ridiculous this was. They were on a mattress on top of a heap of rubbish. They had very nearly drowned in it. And she was introducing herself as if they had just met in the school playground – and telling him she was from Finland! He must think she was stark, staring bonkers. But, of course, he couldn't understand her.

Then he stood up on the mattress and shouted something – it sounded like 'Rodrigo' – and stepped off it into the rubbish.

'No!' she cried in alarm, reaching out for him with both arms.

He paused and looked over his shoulder at her. An expression of surprise crossed his face. Then he said,

'Come,' and set off without a backward glance.

She watched him walk away from her. He was stumbling, almost floundering, in the rubbish but he wasn't sinking into it.

'Wait for me,' she cried and scrambled off the mattress.

She struggled in his wake, sinking up to her knees at times, but there was a solidity to it – a density – that had not been there before. It was like walking down a sand dune, not sinking in a bog.

Then the slope began to level out and though the filth was all around her she was no longer wading through it. The ground felt solid under her feet. She could see things in detail now, things she would far rather not have seen. The skull of a small animal that could have been a cat, the dried-out carcass of a crow, a dead dog crawling with maggots that she nearly stepped in. She looked at the boy as if to share the horror but he was unconcernedly brushing himself down and scratching inside his shirt. She realized how unspeakably dirty he was. Then she looked down at herself and saw she was almost as bad. She felt itchy all over. Her scalp felt as if it was alive with crawling things. She shuddered and reached up, frantically ruffling her hair with both hands, dreading to think what foul, disgusting creatures had attached themselves to her. Then the flies found them. A great buzzing cloud, dropping out of the sky or rising from the ground, you couldn't tell which; they were everywhere. She flapped her hands at them and cried out in rage and revulsion.

This was the most disgusting place on Earth.

But perhaps it wasn't *on* Earth. It was more like Hell.

People said Hell didn't exist. Even church people said it didn't exist. But if this wasn't Hell, what kind of place was it?

She looked around for the boy, her only companion in this horror. But he was no longer alone. He was surrounded by other children – boys and girls. They were all shouting at him in the language she couldn't understand, grinning and slapping his back as if he'd done something remarkable. None of them took any notice of her. She might not have been there. Then he was shouting back at them and pointing at the heap of rubbish and their expressions changed. They began to scramble up it, digging into it with their bare hands and throwing it back over their shoulders, like dogs digging for a bone.

She ran up to the boy. 'What are you doing?' she yelled. 'You'll have it down on us again.'

He turned and stared at her and she realized he couldn't understand, so she started to wave her hands wildly in front of his face in a gesture that meant *stop* in any language in the world.

But whether or not it meant anything to him, he ignored her and carried on digging.

'What's the matter with you?' she said. 'Are you crazy?'

Then she remembered the other boy. The boy who had been with him when the tip had started to slide. He was buried under tons of rubbish. And there was no life raft to save him.

She felt her legs go weak and she sank to her knees and began to shake with sobs.

She knew she must be in shock. She couldn't stop shaking and sobbing.

Get me out of here, she thought.

But there was no end to the nightmare.

There was a roaring, crunching, grinding noise and something was lumbering out of the haze of heat and dust towards her, a great, yellow monster with glaring eyes and gaping jaws, belching smoke.

She opened her mouth to scream but no sound

would come. She couldn't move her legs. Then she realized. It was a bulldozer! Headlights glaring through the dust, smoke pouring out of the overhead exhaust – and a giant blade or scoop at the front. The driver leaned out of his cab and shouted up at the children crawling on the tip.

The boy turned and shouted something back and then they all scattered as the machine lurched towards them, straight into the mountain of rubbish. The huge mechanical jaw took a great bite out of it, lifted it high in the air, swung round and dumped it on the ground. Like a monster vomiting up its entrails. A great stream of filth. But no boy.

The driver wrestled with the levers. The engine roared, the exhaust belched more smoke. A great grinding of gears, the huge iron tracks climbing and crunching over the rubbish in its path and the mechanical jaws moving up and down, up and down . . .

But it did not find the missing boy – or his body.

The children sat in a silent huddle on the ground, watching, their eyes dull with despair or indifference, it was hard to tell. And then the driver shouted something at them, tapped at his watch and backed off, lifting the huge blade for the last time. Then the machine turned in its own length and trundled away in a cloud of dust.

Jade became aware of the boy standing next to her.

'What did he say?' she asked him. 'Has he gone for help?'

'No,' said the boy. 'He go for work.'

She did not understand him at first. Then it dawned on her.

The driver had gone back to his work.

'But what about your friend?' she demanded wildly.

The boy shrugged.

'Is gone,' he said. 'Dead. *Terminado*. Is one of us. *Los Perdidos*.'

Los Perdidos. She was to hear that word many times over the next few days. Uttered sometimes with a shrug of resignation, sometimes with a kind of defiant pride. The Lost Ones. *Los Chicos Perdidos* – the Lost Children, who lived off the waste others threw away.

If you could call it living.

They were scavengers. They scoured the dump for cloth, plastic, glass – anything that could be salvaged or recycled and sold to *Los Patrones*, the bosses, the dealers in waste products. On an average day they made three or four *quetzales* – about half a US dollar. A quarter of what it cost for a Big Mac at McDonald's in Guatemala City. But *Los Perdidos* were not in the habit of dining at McDonald's. They ate what they found on the tip, or a handful of rice and beans heated up on a primitive stove or an open fire. And if they were lucky and found something of value – a piece of cutlery, say, or costume jewellery thrown away by mistake – they might make enough for some meat to go with it or a can of Coke.

The Lost Ones lived on the dump – in squalid hovels made from the rubbish itself. Whole families of eight, nine, ten people – men, women and children – in a single hut with a tin roof and a dirt floor, for fathers and mothers worked the dump, too, if it was the only work they could find.

But mostly it was work for the children, the *chicos*.

The *chicos*. Jade had never seen anything like them. Not in real life, only in pictures. Like the slum kids of Victorian London: the street urchins in *Oliver Twist* who had to pick a pocket or two. All skin and bone, dressed in filthy rags, their bodies covered in old scars, crusted scabs and running sores, unwashed hair and skin, infested with lice and ringworm. Old eyes staring out of faces she couldn't believe had ever been young. Eyes that had seen too much evil and would see a lot more before they were closed for ever. Constantly shifting, always on the lookout for trouble or opportunity. A truck or a tractor, a shiny piece of glass or jewellery lying among the rubbish, a scrap of food that was just about edible, the vultures in the sky and the dogs on the ground . . . Jade could scarcely think of them as children at all. They were more like sinister little midgets. Stunted adults.

The boy Jade had rescued – Paco – was an orphan. He told Jade he was twelve but she didn't believe him. He looked ten at most. Ten going on forty. For though he was smaller and skinnier than most of his companions he had the look of an ageing sprite, a cunning old goblin with a shock of wiry, black hair and funny little button nose.

He lived in a hut with four other *chicos* who were without parents and who called him *El Jefe*, the chief. They were all older and bigger than him but he was their natural leader. The Artful Dodger. The one who organized their villainies and got the best deals with *Los Patrones*. The one they relied upon to outwit their enemies.

They had many enemies. There were the other gangs of course, who fought them for the best pitch and the best pickings when the rubbish trucks arrived from the wealthier parts of the city. There were *Los Patrones* who tried to cheat them and pay as little as possible for the little they had to sell. There were the bulldozer and the tractor drivers who would run them down like vermin if they didn't see them in the dirt and the dust. And then there were the true vermin: the other creatures who competed for the waste of Guatemala City. The vultures and the dogs and the rats. These hunted in gangs, too, and they had their gang leaders who were as tough and violent, as ruthless and cunning as any human.

Jade got to know them well over the next few days: the first days of her new life on the tip. The vultures were led by a loathsome creature called *El Monstro* – the monster – because he was bigger and uglier than any of the others. Jade had thought vultures only went for dead things but this didn't seem to be true. Not of the vultures on the dump. They had vicious, cruel beaks that could slice into living flesh as easily as they could rip up the dead and they'd fight the *chicos* for scraps of food among the rubbish. They'd even been known to go for the babies and toddlers who were too young to work and who played in the puddles and the filth outside the hovels.

Los Perdidos carried sticks to beat them off – even a skinny little runt like Paco could beat off the average vulture with a stick – and they would rarely attack a large gang. But *El Monstro* would circle high in the sky, searching for some lone kid searching among the rubbish, and then he'd swoop down low over his head, raking him with his sharp talons. Again and again he'd dive down, cutting the flesh to the bone and if the kid fell to the ground, swooning from loss of blood, the rest of the vile breed would come down and make an end to him.

But the rats were even worse. There was one in particular, he wasn't big or strong – like Paco he was smaller than most of the other rats in his pack with a funny little patch of hair under his throat, like a ruff – but he was possessed of a wicked cunning. *Los Perdidos* called him *El Diablo*, the Devil.

The *chicos* laid traps for the rats – and ate them if they caught them. A dead rat, barbecued on a spit, was often the only meat they had in days or even weeks. But *El Diablo* laid traps for the *chicos*. He knew all the places that were dangerous to humans – the mounds of rubbish that were least stable and prone to collapse, often because the rats had undermined them with their tunnels, and he would lure the *chicos* on to them. He would find a piece of jewellery or brightly coloured glass among the rubbish and carry it in his mouth and drop it in clear view halfway up one of the tips that was liable to slide. There was a fair chance that if one or more of the kids climbed up to reach this treasure the whole thing would come down on them and bury them alive.

Then *El Diablo* and his rat pack would have a feast.

Paco blamed *El Diablo* and *El Monstro* personally for the death of Rodrigo: *El Diablo* for undermining the tip and *El Monstro* for the fight over the pizza that had caused it to slide. And he knew the rats would be feasting on the body under the mound of rubbish.

It was doing his head in. Not because he had any deep feelings for Rodrigo, Jade realized. Life was cheap on the dump. People died all the time. Or disappeared. One day they were there; the next they were gone. No one reported them missing or did very much about it. But Paco cared about what had happened to Rodrigo because Rodrigo had been one of his own. He had been under Paco's protection and Paco couldn't bear the idea that Death had snatched him away, right from under his nose. It was disrespectful, a challenge to his power. And if he couldn't be revenged on Death he was going to take it out on the nearest things to it.

Which were the rats and the vultures.

He lay awake at night brooding over it and plotting his revenge.

All the kids respected Paco for his cunning – but he had something more than that, something that made people fear him, even the older kids and the adults on the dump, and it took Jade a little while to figure out what it was.

In the meantime she had something more important to worry about. For within a few minutes of meeting Paco and the other *chicos* she had discovered something rather alarming about herself.

She had concluded, with numbing certainty, that she was dead.

12

The Child of Fire

She had to be dead; it was the only thing that made any sense.

She had crashed into a stone wall on a motorbike. This would make most people dead – or severely mangled.

Then there was the sense of passing into another world. And at the same time of passing *through* it – of not having a proper part in it. Like a ghost.

There was a sense of unreality. Of jumping forward and backwards in time and space. Of moving from place to place without any apparent effort of will or sense of control. Of never knowing where you were or how you got there or why you wanted to be there in the first place.

But the main reason for feeling dead was that no one could see her. Or hear her. Or touch her.

Except Paco.

As far as everyone else was concerned she was simply not there. Or if she was, they made a pretty convincing display of ignoring her.

They looked straight through her.

They even *walked* straight through her.

'Excuse me,' she said, the first time it happened. 'Hello-o!'

The next time she gave them a sharp dig in the ribs with her elbow – and got absolutely zilch reaction.

After that she gave up.

'Don't mind me,' she said. 'I'm not here.'

This could be quite frightening of course. It made you feel confused about where you really were – or *who* you were.

Of course a part of her clung to the belief that this was just a game. *The* game. But it was still scary because it *felt* like being dead. And she wouldn't have been surprised to find that Being Dead was a necessary condition of playing the game. Something Kobal had written into the programme – but failed to mention to her.

If it hadn't been for Paco she'd have gone crazy.

But at least Paco knew she was there. She could even have a conversation with him — of sorts. It wasn't like a normal conversation. It was more like a conversation in a dream. She wasn't conscious of his lips moving but she knew he was talking to her and she could understand what he was saying.

This scared her, too, for she had never been able to get used to reading other people's thoughts. And besides, it was different with Paco. It wasn't like it was with other people; it felt more instinctive than that. It was as if she was a part of him.

Then, when he told her where he came from and what had happened to his parents, she began to realize why this might be the case.

His mother came from a remote village in the interior but she had been forced to flee because of the fighting. There was always fighting in Guatemala, Paco told Jade, as if it was something to be proud of. She fled to the United States as an illegal immigrant and eventually arrived in New York City where she met someone. A doctor, she told Paco, a man of substance. But he did something illegal — Paco thought it was some kind of operation that went wrong — and he was sent to jail. By this time Paco's mother was pregnant with Paco — and before they took the doctor away he gave her some money to go back home. He said in seven years, when he had served his sentence, he would come and find her. She and the child. In the meantime, as long as she obeyed his instructions, he would make sure they were provided for.

'This doctor,' said Jade, 'did your mother say what he was like?'

Paco shrugged. 'Only that he was a gringo – and very rich. But she *would* say that, wouldn't she?'

Even so, his mother didn't seem short of money. They lived in a house near an old Mayan temple on the slopes of a volcano.

'An old *what* temple?' Jade had not heard of the Mayans. They were the people who had lived in Guatemala before the Spaniards came, Paco told her, and the temple was one of the places where they sacrificed their victims as an offering to the Sun God, Kinish Ahau.

'They *sacrificed* people?' Jade stared at him in horror, not entirely sure what he meant.

'You wanna know how?' said Paco, grinning.

Jade wasn't sure she did, but Paco told her anyway. With great relish.

'They dragged them up a long flight of stairs to the altar where the priest was waiting for them with a knife. And he cut out their heart while it was still beating and burned it on an open fire.'

'I don't believe you,' said Jade. 'Why would he *do* that?'

'I told you – it was a sacrifice. To Kinish Ahau. They thought it was the only way they could make the sun rise in the morning. Otherwise it might go away and the world would come to an end.'

'How do you know all this?' demanded Jade suspiciously.

'Because my mother was a tour guide,' said Paco, 'and that's the story she told them.'

Paco and his mother lived at the temple until he was nearly seven – and then the *bandidos* came.

'They came to rob the tourists,' said Paco, 'but then they got drunk and started shooting everything that moved.'

One of the people they shot was his mother. Paco found her body, in the ruins of their house. Then he ran away and came to the dump. It had been his home for two years when Jade met him. Rubbish Dump Number Three, Guatemala City.

'And did you never see your father again?' Jade asked him when he had finished this story. 'The doctor?'

Paco shook his head.

Jade had an idea who the doctor was, of course. And if she was right this would make Paco her little brother. Or, at least, her half-brother. And that must be why she was here. Kobal had sent her to find him.

Although they did not look alike, they did have one thing in common.

Paco could read people's thoughts.

At least, Jade *thought* he could.

She couldn't tell for sure but he had a certain way of looking at people which she knew was a bit like the way *she* sometimes looked at people – as if receiving some kind of a message or signal. She knew people were afraid of him. They would look away as if they were unable to meet his eyes.

He had some kind of inner power – and although it didn't work on Jade (another reason for thinking she was dead) she knew how other people felt. They felt like they were staring into the sun. And if they stared too long, even for just a few seconds, it would burn them up. It would bore right into their skulls and burn up their brain cells like a laser.

This was the power Paco had. But he didn't know how to use it yet. He might not even know he had it. He just thought he was naturally clever and that he could often make people do what he wanted them to do.

But not animals. Not rats or vultures.

'I'm going to get them,' he kept saying. 'I'm going to make them pay.'

But how?

While Paco plotted his revenge, Jade worried about how she was going to get them both out of here. For surely that was the point of the game.

Unless it wasn't a game and she really was dead.

She wracked her brains over this. She wandered all over the dump in the hope that somehow she would find her way back to the clearing in the middle of the forest but it was no use. The dump seemed to go on for ever.

In fact it was probably the size of five or six football pitches, bounded by a tall wire fence shot full of holes and gaps but topped with barbed wire. And within this vast compound were hundreds of individual heaps of rubbish each about twenty or thirty metres high and growing. Every day the trucks came in from the various zones of the city and tipped out more waste. The air was thick with dust. People could hardly breathe in it and all of the municipal workers wore masks. Even the *chicos* wore rags wrapped round their faces most of the time. And it was blisteringly hot. The heat rose in waves from the ground . . .

And the smell. The smell was just indescribable.

Even if she was a ghost all of Jade's senses seemed to be functioning perfectly. She baked in the heat and choked in the dust and the smell made her want to throw up.

She looked like all the other *chicos* now. And smelled like them too. And her eyes were always on the lookout for trouble, sliding to right and left and then suddenly darting up to the sky to check on the vultures.

She hated the vultures more than the rats and she hated the dogs more than either of them. Hated and feared them.

The dogs roamed the dump in packs. Six or seven to a pack. Loathsome creatures, mangy and covered in sores but with savage teeth and wicked eyes. It was mainly on account of the dogs that the *chicos* carried sticks. And usually the dogs kept out of their way. But sometimes, when there was food to be had they would attack with a savagery that Jade found more frightening than anything else on the dump.

They could see her, too. Or if they couldn't see her

they could sense her. They would turn towards her with their hackles raised and their black lips would draw back from their teeth and they'd snarl and back away, stiff-legged. She was always very careful to keep out of their way. She had a feeling they were just waiting for the opportunity to have a go at her.

There was one in particular, one of the pack leaders: a large black hound with more than a hint of Dobermann in him. The *chicos* called him *El Capitan*. She would look up sometimes and find him looking down at her from the top of a heap of rubbish with his tongue lolling and a certain look in his eye, like he was measuring her for a coffin. He was like her personal demon dog, her Hound of the Baskervilles.

But with Paco it was *El Diablo*. He was obsessed with the creature, as if they were locked in some kind of leadership contest. Jade could tell he was always thinking about him and how to get the better of him.

'Can't you just use rat poison?' she said.

Paco gave her a look that would have killed several million brain cells if she hadn't been immune.

Rat poison was used all the time in the dump. It was used by the municipal workers; it was even used in some of the shacks. And it killed a lot of rats. But it couldn't kill *El Diablo*. Not according to Paco. *El*

Diablo could smell rat poison a mile away. Even poison that didn't smell. According to Paco, if *El Diablo* found a piece of food with rat poison on it he fell about laughing. Then he peed on it – just to let you know he'd been there.

El Diablo knew that *Los Perdidos* didn't leave food lying around – and that if they did the chances were that it was poisoned.

'But what if you put it on something else,' Jade mused, 'something that wasn't food.'

'Brilliant,' said Paco – or words to that effect. 'But if it's not food how is he going to eat it? And if he doesn't eat it, how is he going to get poisoned? Dumbo.'

But Jade was remembering something Paco had told her about *El Diablo*.

And something Kobal had told her about fighting a war.

First know thine enemy, Kobal had said.

'What about jewellery?' she said.

Paco stared at her as if she'd totally lost it.

'You mean the kind of jewellery he wears to go to the rats' ball?' he said.

'I mean the kind of jewellery he picks up in his mouth,' Jade said coolly, 'and leaves around where one of you halfwits can find it and get buried alive.'

Paco stared at her some more. Then he slapped the side of his head with the heel of his hand.

'Exactly,' said Jade. 'Dumbo.'

The poison was easy. Paco sent his boys off. Within minutes they'd come back with a whole tin of poison from the municipal stores. *Odourless and tasteless* it said on the label.

But the jewellery was more of a problem.

The Lost Ones didn't go in for wearing jewellery as a rule.

Nor did the municipal workers.

Paco didn't want to hang around for several days until a piece of jewellery turned up on the dump. The only alternative seemed to be to go to one of the downtown shopping areas and snatch a necklace from some unsuspecting female. But there was a certain amount of risk attached to this and Paco was not into taking risks, not if he could help it.

He wasn't against stealing – far from it – but he preferred to arrange things so there was very little chance of being caught.

The best option, he decided, was the school.

The school had been started a year back by some volunteers from *El Norte*, especially for the children of the dump. Students from all over the world came to work at the school during their summer holidays to give *Los Perdidos* some basic education. Of course if the kids were at lessons they couldn't earn any money on the dump, so to encourage them the school gave them a free meal at midday.

Paco was quite keen on the school, partly because of the free meal but also because it had a computer he could use. And the teachers were quite keen on Paco, even if he was a pain at times, because he could read and write and even speak a little English. They said he was bright enough to go to university some day, if only he knuckled down to some serious studies.

Paco had his own opinions on this but if the teachers could be of some use to them he'd use them. The same as he used everybody else. And in this case they could provide him with the bait for *El Diablo*.

There was one particular teacher he had in mind. Her name was Amy and she often wore jewellery to school. Nothing special, just a ring or two and a cheap necklace made of beads or glass. But it would do for Paco's purposes.

Although Amy wore the jewellery when she arrived at the school she very rarely wore it in class. Maybe she had noticed the way some of *Los Perdidos* were looking at it. Paco reckoned she kept it in her desk.

So the next day when he and the other *chicos* went to school he arranged a little diversion. Two of the boys started a fight at the back of the class. This was not unusual. The boys were always fighting and the teachers were always having to break them up.

Usually if it happened in class and not in the playground it was enough to just yell at them to quit. Which Amy did. But this time the boys kept on slugging it out and Amy had to run in and pull them apart. And while she was at the back of the class yelling and heaving at them and they were spitting at clawing at each other like a pair of wildcats, Paco was at the front of the class helping himself to the contents of her desk.

Later he showed Jade the result. A cheap leather necklace threaded with bright-red beads.

Jade felt bad about this but she reckoned that if she could get rid of *El Diablo* she'd be doing everyone a favour. He and his slimy friends were just as much of a pest in the school as they were in the rest of the dump. But she didn't need the whole necklace. She untied the knot at the back and slid four of the beads off the leather thong. Then she tied it up again and gave it to Paco to put back in the teacher's desk in the morning.

He stared at her in disbelief and opened his mouth to argue.

'Don't argue,' she said. 'Just do it.'

Paco closed his mouth like a rat-trap and put the necklace in his pocket.

Jade threaded each of the beads on a piece of string and dipped them in the tin of rat poison. Then she let them dry in the sun.

Paco reckoned it was better if Jade distributed them around the dump rather than him or one of the other *chicos*. He had realized, of course, that nobody else could see her. And if she was invisible to *Los Perdidos* she must be invisible to the rats.

Jade wasn't so sure about this. And there was another problem that had just occurred to her.

What if some of the *chicos* saw the beads before *Il Diablo*?

Paco had already thought of this and he had the answer. There was a part of the dump *Los Perdidos* called Rats' Alley – a long, narrow passage between two great mounds of rubbish, right in the middle of the dump. These particular heaps had been worked over a long time ago for anything of value so people hardly ever went there. But you did get loads of rats. Paco reckoned something big had died there – maybe something human – and was buried under the rubbish. It was the perfect place for leaving the beads, he said.

Great, said Jade. But it had been her idea so reluctantly she agreed. She wrapped the beads in a bit of tissue and set out across the dump with Paco following at a discreet distance.

She had never come across Rats' Alley before in all her wanderings and she didn't like the look of it. It was a deep gully with mounds of rubbish rising up on either side like twin peaks. Ominously quiet and in deep shadow. She couldn't see any rats but that meant nothing. Experience had taught her that the rats were everywhere. She looked up and saw the vultures circling. But they were high enough not to be a problem.

She stooped down at the entrance to the passage and pretended to be tying the laces on her trainers while she slid one of the beads out of the tissue and dropped it on the ground. Then she walked on for a bit and did it again. She was now deep in the middle of the dump with the heaps of rubbish towering above her. She should have been used to this by now but she was uneasy. It didn't feel right. She had never felt so alone on the dump. Every nerve ending told her something was wrong, that she was walking into a trap. She looked back for Paco. No sign of him. She couldn't see the way out either. It looked like a dead end.

She looked up at the sky. The vultures were still there but at a safe distance. She walked on and knelt down to drop the last bead. Then she saw the rat.

It was sitting in the middle of the path, watching her, stroking its whiskers with its paws. She could have sworn it was grinning at her.

She saw the little ruff of hair at its throat.

El Diablo.

But did he know what she was doing? Just how clever *was* he?

She stared at him. What is your worst fear, you little rat, she thought? But she couldn't tell. She was no good with animals.

Then she heard a sound. A sound that made the hairs rise on the back of her neck. And she knew why *El Diablo* was grinning at her.

She had kept her eye on the vultures but she had forgotten the dogs.

13

Brother Benedict

'*This is where they killed the children.*'

The woman Jade knew as Aunt Em looked up sharply from the *A–Z* she had been consulting. Then she looked down because the voice seemed to be coming from ground level. Sure enough, her startled gaze met that of a man in a hooded jacket sitting on the pavement with a neat handwritten sign in front of him that read: *Gnosher and His Friend Thank You for Your Kindness.*

Next to him, with its long black muzzle resting on its paws, lay a dog. Gnosher – or His Friend?

Emily looked quickly away, not wishing to become involved in a conversation with someone who was clearly one stop short of Barking.

'It's true,' he said in a reasonable tone. 'It used to be a prison. For women and children. Lots of the kids died. We're probably standing on their graves. Except that I'm sitting,' he added reflectively. 'And they probably just threw the bodies in the river, anyway.'

Emily looked at him again. He didn't sound mad and he had quite an educated voice. But he certainly looked a bit odd. She couldn't see much of his features because he had his hood up and he wore shades – in February. She fished in the pocket of her raincoat for some loose change and dropped it into the cap.

'Thank you, lady,' he said in a different kind of voice. 'Say thank you to the kind lady, Gnosher.'

'Thank you, lady,' said the dog.

Emily looked at the dog and then at the man.

A joker, she thought. With a gift for ventriloquism.

'Talented dog,' she said.

'Oh, there's no end to his talents,' said the man. 'Quite creepy at times. You look as if you're lost.'

He was right. Emily *was* lost. She had arranged to meet the mystery monk – Brother Benedict – at an address he had given her in Victoria but though it was in the *A–Z* she had been unable to locate it in the warren of back streets between the station and the cathedral.

'I was looking for Tothill Street,' she said uncertainly, not sure if she should pursue the conversation.

'Well, look no further,' he said. 'You've found it.'

'Really?' Emily glanced back towards the street sign at the corner. She couldn't quite see it from here but she could have sworn it had said something different.

'It's no longer called that,' said the man. 'It's called Percy Street. But it's still Tothill Street, if you see what I mean. What number did you want?'

'I wasn't given a number,' Emily confessed. 'Just a name.' She felt herself sinking into a bog, or falling down a hole like Alice in Wonderland. Any moment now and she'd see the white rabbit or the Mad Hatter. But in for a penny in for a pound . . . 'The convent of St Mary and St Joseph,' she said.

The man jerked his head up and to the right, like a twitch.

'Right behind you, madam,' he said. 'Used to be the prison.'

Emily looked up at the tall, rather grim building that appeared to run the length of the street. It *looked* like a prison. There were even bars on the windows – on the ground floor at least.

'Good heavens,' she said faintly.

'More like Hell,' said the man, 'And nothing good about it at all. The door's just down there.'

He jerked his head again and she saw a red-painted door a little way down the street.

'Thank you,' she said. She wondered if she'd given him enough money but it was all the change she had and a ten-pound note seemed excessive.

'Well . . . good luck,' she said, moving on.

'And to yourself,' said he. 'You may need it more than I do.'

There was a hint of mockery in his voice – in fact it had been there throughout their conversation – but she let it pass.

Strange man, she said to herself as she walked on.

There was a small brass nameplate with an intercom set into the brickwork beside the door. *Convent of St Mary and St Joseph* it said. But you could easily have missed it. She looked back to give the man a smile of appreciation but he was nowhere to be seen.

'Strange,' she said again, aloud this time. But then she shrugged and rang the bell.

'Yes?' A woman's voice.

Emily put her face close to the intercom.

'Dr Emily Mortlake,' she said. 'For Brother Benedict.'

The only response was a buzzing noise from the vicinity of the door. Emily pushed it open and went in.

The man and the dog watched from the shadow of a doorway at the end of the street.

'Well, well, well,' said the man to the dog. 'Here's a turn up for the book.'

He fished inside his jacket and produced a mobile phone – an expensive one with loads of extras. He pressed the quick dial.

'You were right,' he said. 'She came. She's in.'

Emily entered what was presumably the reception area. Opposite her were two painted statues – presumably of St Mary and St Joseph – and a large vase of white lilies which she could tell at a glance were artificial. It was like a Chapel of Repose. Along the wall to her right was a bench, or church pew, for the mourners. On her left a glass partition.

'Yes?' said a voice. 'Can I help you?'

The voice seemed to come from behind the glass partition although there didn't seem to be anyone there. Emily stepped right up to it. Sitting on a chair, just below the level of the glass, was a very small woman, possibly a dwarf, with white hair and thick glasses. She was knitting a scarf – a long red scarf that reached to the floor and a good way along it and had *Arsenal FC* written on it in white lettering.

'Excuse me,' said Emily, 'but I have an appointment with Brother Benedict. My name is Emily Mortlake.'

'Up the stairs, second door on the right,' said the woman, without stopping work. *Clickety click* went the needles.

Up the stairs, second door on the right.

Emily knocked and entered a large room that could have been a library. Certainly it had enough books. They filled two of the walls. On the third was a grimy window overlooking the street. On the fourth a framed photo of the Pope and two paintings, one of which Emily had seen before. It was called *The Massacre of the Innocents* by Peter Paul Rubens: the slaughter of the children of Jerusalem by King Herod in the days after the birth of Christ.

'*This is where they killed the children.*'

She recalled the words of the man in the street but dismissed them as coincidence. The other painting showed an army of Crusader knights charging across what looked like a frozen lake. The only odd thing about this was that instead of wearing the traditional white with a red cross, like all the other pictures of Crusaders she had ever seen, the tunics of the knights and the trappings of the horses were black – with a white cross.

The door opened and a man came in.

'Dr Mortlake,' he said with a grin. 'I'm Brother Benedict.'

She blinked. He was nothing like she had imagined. Much younger with short blond hair and film-star good looks. Not a hint of a tonsure. And he wore a black leather jacket with jeans and a black T-shirt.

'I'm sorry,' she said. She had been staring at him as if stunned while he stood there with his hand held out. She shook it a little weakly. 'I was expecting something a bit more monk-like,' she said.

'Brown habit and a cowl? Rosary beads? Leather sandals?'

'Something like that,' she confessed.

'We keep that for more formal occasions,' he said. 'Though in our case it's black.'

'I'm sorry?' She sank into the bog again. 'What's black?'

'The habit. Please, do have a seat . . .' There was a long conference table down the centre of the room with about a dozen chairs. 'Can I get you a drink – coffee, tea . . .?'

Emily shook her head.

'Jade,' she said firmly.

'Ah.' He sat down at the table and nodded as if to remind himself. 'Jade.'

'If you know something you have a clear duty—'

He had been stroking his chin with his hand and now he raised a finger in a gentle reproach.

'I didn't say I knew something. I said we had an interest in the case. And that it might be useful to share notes.'

'What "interest"? And she's not a "case", she's a child. And when you say "we" . . .?' She was close to losing her temper.

'I mean the Church.' She made a sound like a small explosion to let him know she wasn't impressed. 'Our particular branch of it, then,' he added. He seemed amused.

'Which is?

'The official title is: the Knights of the Order of the Holy—'

'*Knights?*'

'I suppose "warrior monks" would be more accurate. Founded in Jerusalem during the—'

'*Warrior monks!*' Even more ridiculous. She jerked her head at the painting of the charging knights. 'That lot?'

He looked over his shoulder.

'Ah yes. "That lot" as you put it. We gave up the horses a while back.'

'Lucky horses.' She sat down across the table from him. 'So, getting back to Jade . . .'

'First we need to know something of the background to the c—' He caught the glint in her eye . . . 'The child's background.'

'No,' she corrected him. 'First we need to know what it's got to do with the Knights of the Holy Whatsit.'

'Right.' He sighed. 'There is a man by the name of Kobal. Kirk Kobal, alias Stanislaus Kobalski, alias . . .' He shrugged. 'Well, he has many names. But he was once known as Brother Boris of the Order of—'

'You're kidding me. Kobal was a *monk*?'

He smiled a little grimly. 'I take it you are acquainted with Brother Boris.'

'Not as such but yes, I know Kobal. Or *knew* him.' She shuddered. It wasn't theatrical. She felt like someone had walked over her grave. 'But a monk . . .? When did he fit that into his busy schedule? Before or after he was certified insane?'

'He was quite young at the time. You met him at Houndwood Hospital, I believe?'

'Yes. You know Houndwood?'

'Not from personal experience. I know *of* it. A prison hospital, I believe, for the criminally insane.'

'Quite. Kobal spent two years there. As a patient.' She shook her head in disbelief. 'A monk? Oh, well, I suppose he liked dressing up in the robes.'

'Only on formal occasions,' he reminded her.

'Yes. Still . . . I knew him as a scientist. An expert in the study of the human genome – the secret of human life. Unfortunately he was also mad. I know this is not a medical term but sometimes it just about hits the nail on the head.'

'*Is* there a medical term – for his condition?'

'It was a complicated case. He was not exactly co-operative. He treated psychiatrists with contempt. You could say he was a delusional control freak with a monumental ego.'

'You could say that of most world leaders.'

'Possibly. But most don't actually think they're God. Or the Devil. Or at least they don't make the mistake of telling people.'

'Is that what he really thought?'

She sighed. 'Who knows what he really thought? This is Kobal. Put it this way: he felt he was in the same *category* as God. Superhuman. With a moral mission to improve on the original creation. Unfortunately his plans went considerably beyond the law. He experimented with . . . well, I won't go into the details but it was sufficient to land him in Houndwood. But the man was a genius.' She said this with some bitterness. 'I imagine people said that about Hitler and Stalin but . . . certain aspects of his work – the legitimate stuff – were considered to be so important he was allowed to continue with them – under strict supervision. They built him a special laboratory and gave him a team of researchers. I was one of them.'

He was watching her carefully but she had an idea that this information was not entirely new to him.

'Our work was with inherited diseases. It would have been of immense benefit to . . . humankind. Unfortunately – I'm sorry I keep saying this but a lot of things about Kobal are unfortunate – for the rest of us – Kobal continued with his own work, on the side. Creating the perfect human being. A modest ambition. Super intelligent, super fit, endowed with almost superhuman qualities . . . Flawless. Unlike the ones God had made. Anything you can do . . .'

She put a hand to her forehead and massaged it gently.

'I'm sorry if this is painful for you . . .' he said, but she flapped a hand as if at a troublesome fly.

'One of the women in Houndwood – one of the patients – was discovered to be pregnant. Kobal had been treating her for some woman's complaint. We drew the obvious conclusions but no . . . The egg wasn't hers. It had been planted inside her – by Kobal. For reasons we never quite understood she had agreed to carry it into labour. As a surrogate. That's what she told us, anyway.'

'What did Kobal say?'

'Nothing. He wasn't there. He'd done a bunk.'

'Escaped? From Houndwood? I thought it was a top-security prison.'

'*Hospital*. It is. But Kobal escaped. Another of his talents. Having left a little gift behind for humankind.'

'So he was the father?'

'Well, I wouldn't put it quite like that, would you? But I think we can assume he had fertilized the egg with his own seed. He was creating a new breed of human. A superhuman. No one else would be good enough.'

'And the egg?'

She shook her head. 'We don't know. Donated probably. By someone he had singled out as having the necessary "qualities".'

'But if he was in Houndwood . . .?'

'We were running a laboratory. We had regular deliveries of medical supplies, whatever was needed for our work. He had access to a computer. He could use the Internet, emails . . . I don't suppose he had any problem finding donors. There are enough women out there who would be chuffed as Hell to know they were helping to breed a race of superhumans. And with none of the hassle of bringing them up.'

'Tell me about this woman who had the baby. The surrogate.'

She put her hand to her head again.

'I'm sorry . . . This is all . . . It brings it all back. She was a witch. She thought she was the reincarnation of Morgan-la-Fey — the witch in King Arthur who had his child: Mordred — was that his name? There were other . . . delusions. She thought she was a Druid — the priests of the Ancient Britons before the Romans came. They used to worship trees, I think. Oak trees. And they went in for human sacrifice. I believe they used to chop their victims into pieces and feed them to the trees. Another crackpot religion . . . I'm sorry. I didn't mean yours.'

He didn't seem the least bothered.

'And why was she in Houndwood?'

'She murdered her baby . . . Sorry – sacrificed her.'

She should stop saying *sorry*. And *unfortunate*. It was a condition of knowing Kobal.

Brother Benedict was staring at her. For once she seemed to have cracked his composure. 'She murdered her own baby? And this was the woman . . .'

'That Kobal chose as a surrogate mother for his child. Yes.'

'But even Kobal . . .'

'Maybe he thought she had other "qualities".'

He rubbed both hands wearily across his face. His looked older suddenly.

'Where was she from?'

'She was a local. She came from Rackthorne. The local village.'

'In the Forest of Windsor.'

'Is it? I suppose it is. Lots of oak trees.'

116

'The place where three paths meet.'

'If you say so. Anyway, she had the baby. A baby girl . . .'

'Jade.'

She nodded. 'Why am I telling you this? I'm probably in breach of the Official Secrets Act. I could go to jail. We could both go to jail.'

'I'll take my chance on that.'

His look was challenging.

'Will it get her back?' she demanded.

'I can't promise anything but . . . we'll do our best.'

'You know where Kobal is, don't you?'

He didn't answer.

'The only reason I'm talking to you is—'

'What happened to the child when she was born?'

Emily considered for a moment, wondering how much she could safely tell him. She chose her words with care.

'She was made a ward of court and placed with a couple we thought we could rely on. The woman was an old school friend of mine. I became . . . the godmother. The fairy godmother. I guess I wasn't much good at it, given what happened.'

He said nothing, waiting patiently for her to tell him what had happened. Again she had the feeling that he knew most of it anyway.

'I was looking after her when we were attacked – by some men in masks. Animal masks. We got away. I got her taken to Houndwood where I thought she'd be safe but . . . she went missing. I'd just told her about . . . Kobal. And the circumstances of her birth. That she was the result of some weird "experiment" to improve the human race.'

'How did she take it?'

'Well, as she took off shortly afterwards I think you could say she was fairly upset, don't you? I should never have left her alone.' She regarded him shrewdly. 'Kobal's got her, hasn't he?'

He didn't answer at once. He stood up and went to the window, standing with his back to her.

'I think if he had the power he would want to find her, don't you?' he said. 'And the others.'

'The others?'

He turned sharply as if to catch her unawares.

'His lost children. You knew there were more than one?'

'I . . . We couldn't be sure but . . . we suspected as much. At least – that there was more than one egg.'

'Which he took with him, when he escaped. Frozen in liquid nitrogen.'

How could he know that?

'That was the assumption,' she admitted. 'But—'

'The assumption. Yes. I think we can "assume" that if he wanted to create a new breed of human he would start with more than one, yes? Even God started with two, according to the Bible.'

'Is that what he really wants? To start a new human race?'

'Who know what Kobal really wants? Everything is a game with him. A mystery, wrapped within mysteries. This woman, the surrogate, what happened to her after she had the child?'

'She . . . There were complications with the birth so she was moved to a maternity hospital. Shortly after the birth she disappeared.'

'But not for ever, I think.'

He inclined his head, watching her carefully. The light was behind him and she couldn't see his face very well. Not as well as he could see hers.

'I think you found her,' he said. 'And you know where she is.'

'And if I did, what good would it do?'

'It might help to know why she agreed to carry his child.'

'I don't see why.'

'It might provide a clue to Kobal's motives. To the nature of the game he is playing.'

'And would that help us find Jade?'

'I believe it would.'

'My only concern is Jade,' she said. She looked at him plaintively. 'Do you think she's still alive?'

He came away from the window but he didn't sit down. Now he was staring at the painting on the wall. *The Massacre of the Innocents.*

'At this moment in time,' he said, 'I really have no idea.'

14

The Headless Chickens

Some time in the distant past, when she was eight or nine years old, Jade had started keeping a notebook on how to survive dangerous and life-threatening situations. They were listed alphabetically and included such useful tips as:

A for Air Crash: best places to sit . . .
B for Bears: how to distract with umbrella . . .
C for Cold: How to light fire using broken glass.

Under D for Dogs she had copied the following:

1. Do Not Stroke.
2. If threatened, stare into eyes and back slowly away.

It occurred to her now, as she confronted the

slavering pack of hounds in the middle of Rubbish Dump Number Three, Guatemala City, that so far as advice went, Do Not Stroke fell considerably short of Expert.

In fact Do Not Stroke was probably in the same category as Do Not Put Hand in Mechanical Chip Slicer.

And how did you manage to stare simultaneously into six pairs of eyes?

She had seen the dogs a number of times on the dump. They were a desperate-looking bunch at the best of times: starving, slinking curs, covered in scabs and running sores, with their ribs clearly visible through their mangy, matted hair. But they had one impressive feature. They all had teeth like Rottweilers. Teeth too big for their slobbering mouths. Teeth that had spent a lifetime crunching up tin cans and bones and other assorted debris. Teeth that you definitely did not want to put your hand near. Or any other part of your body.

They advanced on Jade in a pack: stiff-legged, teeth barred and hackles raised. Unlike the contributors to her Survivor's Handbook, Jade was no expert but she knew these were not generally regarded as friendly signs. They were not wagging their tails. She fixed the leader in the recommended stare. It continued to advance. She backed slowly away. It snarled and showed a few more teeth.

Then something — a sound or an instinct — made her look up.

She ducked just in time. The claws missed her by a hair's breadth. She felt the whoosh of wings and an outraged screech filled the foetid air.

El Monstro landed awkwardly and staggered round to confront her, flapping his wings and bobbing his disgusting head on its scrawny neck. Two of his evil comrades landed beside him. They made little hopping runs, flapping their wings and darting their long necks at her. Like snakes with beaks.

The dogs were in a frenzy, furious at these uninvited guests at the feast. But they weren't going to give up. Two or three of them made a rush at the vultures while the others backed Jade up against the tip. There was only one way to go. Up and over. She looked up at the great mound of filth towering above her head.

And there — sitting watching like whiskered spectators at the ringside — were the rats.

El Diablo had been joined by about a score of his gang. They just sat there as if to enjoy the sport. And maybe there'd be a few scraps left over for them when the fight was over.

The horror of it nearly made her pass right out. And that would have been an end to her.

The one thing that saved her was anger. The thought of those loathsome creatures stripping the flesh from her bones made her furious beyond reason. She turned and ran at the rats, screaming with range. Right up the side of the dump.

They stared at her for a moment, as if they couldn't believe it. The victim wasn't supposed to leave the ring. Then they scattered.

Jade was up to her ankles in rubbish but she didn't sink any further. And when the momentum of her charge had gone and the rats had scattered before her she kept going, scrambling on all fours now, in a desperate bid to reach the top of the mound. She knew how *El Diablo* lured his victims on to the tips – she'd seen it happen with little Rodrigo. Any second now and it would start to slide and she'd be buried under tons of filth – trapped in the rats' larder – but she was past caring. And somehow, miraculously, the rubbish held firm beneath her feet.

She'd almost reached the top. She snatched a quick

glance over her shoulder. The dogs were still in a howling, baying pack down below. But the vultures were in the air, climbing for height. More were spiralling down to join them. *El Monstro* tipped his wing like a dive bomber and came screaming down.

She reached the peak . . .

And stood, staring in horror and disbelief at what lay ahead.

It seemed to go on for ever. Mound after mound of rubbish stretching into the distant heat haze. And not another human being in sight.

It couldn't be true. It had to be an illusion.

The vulture swooped. Jade ducked. His outstretched talons took a clump of hair but missed her scalp. He screamed and wheeled for the next strike. Jade plunged down the slope, sobbing in despair, no longer even hoping to escape. And now her feet were sinking into the stuff, up to the knees, deeper . . . Up to her thighs now and still sinking, as if into a bog. But somehow still moving, slowly, as if in a dream and the ground opening at her feet, swallowing her up.

She was sinking into a deep trough but instead of closing over her the rubbish seemed to be rising up and away. And then it wasn't rubbish any more. It had turned into trees. She was running along a path through trees.

She looked back – and there were the dogs. The whole barking, baying pack of them. Whatever else had changed, they were the same foul creatures of the dump and they weren't giving up on their dinner. She saw *El Capitan* out ahead of them, his long tongue dripping with foam. Somehow she found some new strength for her legs. She ran on, lungs bursting, a film of sweat clouding her eyes and a noise in her ears like the beating of wings. Then something dropped out of the sky on top of her. She felt a savage pain in her right shoulder. Something clinging to her, black wings beating at her face. She lashed out. A brief glimpse of glaring eyes and a red curved beak, the vicious hook that tore flesh from bones. It lunged at her eyes . . .

And then it was gone and she was in a clearing and there was the motorbike and sidecar with Kobal in his long leather coat and cap and goggles, revving the throttle.

Vroom, vroom.

'Come on,' he said. 'What's keeping you?'

She hurled herself into the sidecar.

'OK. You're back. Safe and sound.'

But his voice was strangely distant. Muffled. As if it was seeping through a filter and she couldn't see him. She couldn't see anything. The vulture had taken her eyes . . . She was blind.

And then Kobal was standing over her and she was staring up at him. He had the black helmet in his hand. She put her own hand up to her head. Felt her hair. Looked around. No vultures, no rats, no dogs. She was sitting in the sidecar, motionless in the garage and Kobal reaching his hand down to her to help her up.

'I don't know about you,' he said, 'but I'm about ready for a coffee break.'

They stepped out of the lift. Everything was exactly as they had left it. Laurie the bear was scratching his bum against a tree. The fruit bat was hanging upside down from the tree. The cockatoo was preening its feathers. And breakfast was still on the table.

She started at each of them in turn. Then at Kobal.

'How long have I been away?'

He looked at his watch. 'Oh, about ten minutes.'

'Ten minutes! But it was like . . . *days.*'

'It probably was – in the game.'

He sat down at the table by the pool and signalled

Laurie for some fresh coffee. The bear shuffled off in the direction of the kitchens.

Jade sank down in her chair.

'I thought I was dead,' she said.

Kobal seemed to find this amusing.

'You very nearly were,' he said.

'I mean, I *felt* like I was dead – all the time I was there.'

He frowned. 'What does it feel like – being dead?'

She looked at him to see if he was serious. He seemed to be.

'Weird,' she said with a shudder. She didn't think she could describe it.

'Any feelings?'

It was like he was taking notes.

'Well . . .' She tried to remember, while it was still fresh in her mind, like a dream she had just come out of. 'I could see things . . .'

'In colour?'

'I think in colour . . . And I could certainly smell things.'

She still could. The stench of the tip was still in her nostrils. She felt she could smell it on her clothes but when she sniffed at her sleeve it just smelled normal – as if it had been in the wash. And not a stain on her. Even her hands were clean.

'How about hearing?'

She remembered the screech of the vultures, the barking of the dogs, the sound of the bulldozer tearing into the rubbish in search of Rodrigo's body. She nodded.

'Yes, I could hear all right.'

'Touch? Taste?'

Had she touched anything? She looked at her hands again. Spotless. But they'd been filthy on the dump. With a thick layer of grime under her nails. She could remember clawing at the rubbish as she climbed up the tip. Tin cans digging into her palms.

'I could feel things but I'm not sure about tasting. I can't remember eating anything – all the time I was there.'

'Well, that's four senses out of five,' he said. 'Not bad for a dead person.'

'OK, but it still didn't feel like I was really there. And I wasn't, was I? Look at me. I'm clean.'

'You were there – but you weren't there,' he said, as if this made perfect sense. And maybe it did. To him. 'That's why it's so much fun.'

'Fun?' She stared at him. *Fun*?

'Were *you* there?' she demanded.

'Did you see me there?'

'No but . . .' This meant nothing. He could have been in disguise. He could have been *El Diablo*. They had lots in common.

'You knew what was happening to me?'

'Oh yes. Every moment.'

'And you think it was fun?'

'Didn't you? It looked like it was fun.'

It was useless talking to him. He had a different mind from ordinary people. But she had to try.

'The things that were happening to me – and to the other kids – were they real?'

'As real as anything.'

'So – could I have been killed? Like Rodrigo?'

'I guess so,' he said, as if the thought had just occurred to him and he found it vaguely surprising.

'So what would you have done about it? Could you have got me out of it?'

'I did, didn't I?'

'I suppose you did,' she conceded. But she wasn't entirely convinced.

Laurie came back with the coffee on a tray. He was balancing it carefully on one paw and watching it very closely as if daring it to try and get away.

Jade wondered, not for the first time, why Kobal

insisted on using a bear as a house servant. Surely a man or a woman would have been much more practical: someone with hands instead of massive great paws – and claws the size of daggers. He could have got someone from an agency. But Kobal always knew best. She noticed how he watched the bear every step of the way, as if he was willing it to fail.

Somehow Laurie managed to set the tray down with the coffee pot still on it. Kobal poured for himself but Jade wouldn't have any.

'Anything else? Fruit juice. Hot chocolate, cold chocolate. Lours will fetch it for you.'

Lours was what Kobal called him. French for 'bear', he said. *Laurie* was Jade's idea.

'No thank you,' she said firmly.

'Very well, Lours, you're dismissed,' said Kobal, waving his hand airily. 'Go scratch fleas or find a hive of honey bees or whatever else it is that bears do.'

Jade tried to catch the bear's eye to show her sympathy but he just put his head down and shambled off.

Kobal sat back and poured his coffee. He seemed very pleased with himself. And with Jade, apparently.

'Well, you did the business, babe,' he said.

'What business?' She regarded him with deep suspicion.

'You found the boy. Paco. Your baby brother.'

'So he *was* my brother?'

'Half-brother. Yes. *Fernando*. That's the name I give him, anyway. *Paco*'s the short form, I believe, a kind of nickname. Little Paco. Hasn't grown much, has he?' He frowned. 'I expect it's the diet. Have to feed him up a bit when we get him here.'

'He's coming here?'

'Of course. Now you've found him for us. We traced him as far as the temple but then we lost the scent. Hardly surprising, in a dump like that.'

'*We?*'

'My agents.'

'So . . .' Her head was full of questions. She tried to sort them out in order of priority. 'So he really is in the dump?'

'Rubbish Dump Number Three, Guatemala City. Soon as we've finished here I'll make a call, get my people on to it. Bit of luck we'll have him back by the end of the week.'

'But how . . .'

He was ahead of her. 'How did you find him?' He tapped the side of his head. 'It's all in here.' Then he leaned forward and tapped hers. 'And in there. You've got it, kid. The gift.'

'But what is it?'

'The power,' he replied — as if that explained everything. 'Course, you had a bit of help from the computer. A lot of help, in point of fact.'

He sipped his coffee complacently. She could have thrown it at him. She stood up.

'Where you going?' he said.

'For a walk. I need to clear my head of all this . . . rubbish.'

'Sit down,' he said mildly. He pointed at the chair. She sat.

'OK. I programmed the computer with the information I *did* have. Date of birth, place of birth, name, family background, the DNA footprint . . .' He caught her eye and she knew he'd slipped that in to irritate her but she said nothing . . . 'Other things you don't want to know about. Yet. I knew his mother had taken him to Guatemala, as per instruction . . .'

'His mother? His *real* mother?'

'The host mother. The surrogate. The woman who carried him.'

'So what happened to his real mother? His natural mother. Was she the same as mine?'

133

'No.' He sighed impatiently. 'I told you, he's your half-brother. He had a different mother. Donor, I should say, because all she did was donate an egg. Hardly makes her a mother . . . But we'll leave her out of it for the time being. She's not important. Not any more. She served her purpose. Do you want me to tell you the story or don't you?'

She nodded.

'OK. Then stop interrupting. The *host* mother took him to Guatemala and got herself a job as a tour guide in the Temple of Kinish Ahau, the Mayan god of the sun. The firebird. Who comes in the shape of the macaw.' He looked around as though puzzled. 'I don't think we've got one here. Must make one before Paco gets here. Make him feel at home. So, to continue. Seven years they were supposed to stay there. That was the instruction. But you know something – you can't rely on people. You give them a good income, you provide for them, but can you rely on them?'

'She got killed,' Jade pointed out. 'By bandits.'

'Exactly. And Paco goes AWOL?'

'A-what?'

'Absent Without Leave. And if it hadn't been for you we might never have found him.'

'But how *did* I find him?'

This was what she really wanted to know.

'Well . . . you *could* call it ESP. Extra-sensory perception. But what does it mean? A sixth sense. Something most people don't have. Or have lost the use of. Was a time everybody had it but . . .' He shrugged . . . 'They lost it. Typical human behaviour – they always forget the important things. Only a few people can do it these days.'

'Do *what*?' She nearly stamped her foot in her frustration.

'Communicate with each other, over a long distance. Find each other. Know when something is happening to the other one. Like twins. Some twins anyway. And hens.'

'*Hens?*' She was beginning to lose it. She wondered if *he* was. Some people would say he'd lost it a long time ago.

'Sure. Chickens. Chuck-chucks. The Russians did an experiment with them once. They separated a hen from its chicks and took them off in a submarine.' She stared at him in disbelief. 'A nuclear submarine. Took it hundreds of miles away under the Polar icecap. Then they killed the chickens, one by one. Chopped their heads off. And every time they did the hen went crazy. Ran around in little circles, clucking.'

'But . . . *why*?'

'Because that's what mother hens do when they're distressed.'

'I don't mean the hen. *Aaaagh*. I mean why did *the Russians* do it?'

He looked puzzled. 'They didn't. Russians don't run round in circles clucking. Not as a rule. They sit around making notes. Or playing chess. Or getting drunk.' But then he caught her eye and decided not to push her too far. 'OK. They thought it could be used to send signals – if every other means failed. The point is – the mother hen could *sense* that her chicks were in trouble, even though they were in a submarine under the icecap hundreds of miles away.'

'So – I kind of sensed where Paco was and . . . and in trouble – and I went there?'

'More or less. Except that you didn't *physically* go there. If you want to put a name to it you were an avatar.'

'An avatar?'

'From the Sanskrit *avatāra* – meaning "incarnation". Normally used to describe a divine being who enters the mortal world for a specific time and purpose. Except in your case you entered

Paco's world – in the game.'

'But it *was* a game. It wasn't really happening.'

'Ahh . . . Pass,' he said. 'It *may* have been happening.'

She closed her eyes and counted up to five.

'It's complicated,' he said. 'The important thing is you found him, you communicated with him, and with a bit of luck – because we were reading your thought patterns – we'll find him too.'

She nodded as if she understood.

'And the motorbike?'

'Oh the motorbike was just a bit of fun. To make it seem more real. Like we were really going somewhere.'

She thought of something else that had been bothering her.

'But you drove the motorbike at the wall,' she reminded him. 'And we didn't die. It turned into a forest.'

He grinned – a little smugly. 'An illusion,' he said, 'is all.'

'An illusion?'

'OK. An illusionist shouldn't really explain how he creates his illusions but as you've been so helpful, just this once, I'll break the cardinal rule . . . You saw the beam of the headlight shining on the wall.'

'Ye-es . . .'

'No. What you saw was a projector.'

'A projector?'

'As in *film projector*. You people don't bother much with them any more since the digital revolution but they serve a purpose – if you're an illusionist. Like smoke. And mirrors. And a certain amount of noise, of course, for effect. *Vroom vroom . . .*' He pretended to rev up the throttle . . . 'You were watching a film, is all. We weren't rushing at the wall; the wall was rushing at us. A fast track and a zoom. Then it changed to a forest. And you were in the game.'

She considered this for a moment in silence, looking for flaws, but she couldn't find any. Not offhand.

'So why did you send Paco's mother to Guatemala?'

'I had my reasons,' he said vaguely.

'But he's the only one that was there? In Guatemala.'

'Right. The others are somewhere else.'

'And there's seven altogether. Including me.'

'Uh-huh.'

'Why seven?' This was a question that had been

puzzling her for some time.

'Seven's a good number, don't you think? My lucky number.' He fingered the star round his neck.

'Not very lucky this time, was it,' she pointed out, 'if you lost them – when they were still babies. Or in my case before I was even born.'

He frowned. 'Oh I don't know. Some people would say I was *very* lucky – if they all grew up like you. What have I told you – who does everybody hate?'

'A smartypants,' she said.

'Right. Anyway, I was distracted. People were mucking me about. But now you can find them for me. One down, five to go. Piece of cake for a girl of your talents. If the Enemy doesn't get there first.'

'The Enemy?'

'Yeah. He's on the case. I just heard from one of my agents in London. He's got together with your godmother.'

'Aunt Em?' Her heart leaped. Then she felt a desperate sense of loneliness . . . and longing.

'Aunt Em.' He sneered. Mention of her Aunt Em always seemed to make him especially scornful. Or nervous. 'They think they're going to smoke me out – but I might have a little surprise for them.'

Jade didn't like the sound of that. She sought a means to distract him.

'So – when am I going to look for the rest of the family?'

'Whenever you're ready. Where d'you want to go next? Africa? India? Australia? Hawaii . . .?'

She couldn't help feeling a thrill of anticipation at the thought of playing a new game. She was her father's daughter all right.

'India,' she said.

15

The Witch of Windsor

He was standing outside Baron's Court tube station reading a book. Not a prayer book if the cover was anything to go by. The rush-hour crowds surged around him. Emily watched him through the car windscreen. The sky was overcast and he wore a shiny black jacket with a hood. Even with the hood he still didn't look much like her idea of a monk. He looked up and she waved through the windscreen. His expression didn't change but he walked briskly over and slid into the seat beside her.

'Nice car,' he said.

It was a sports car – an Alfa Spider. She'd hadn't long bought it. She'd wanted one for years but now she was worried about its carbon footprint. This took away a lot of the pleasure of driving it. Her friends would have said this was typical.

'You should get a hybrid,' he said. 'Or one of the new electric cars.'

'Excuse me?'

'If you're worried about the emissions.'

Had she told him that? She didn't think so. Puzzled, she eased the car out into the traffic.

'Course you could get a donkey,' he said. 'but I believe the farting's a problem.' He turned to her with a smile. 'Always something isn't it? *Mea culpa, mea culpa, mea maxima culpa.*'

He made the sign of the cross and fastened his seatbelt.

'How d'you get into this racket?' she asked him as they hit the motorway.

'What particular racket is this?' he enquired mildly.

'The Order of the Holy Whatsit.'

'Oh, that racket. Well, it helps if you're a bloke. But if you're interested you could try with one of the female orders. They're short of nuns these days. Of course being a Catholic is more or less obligatory.'

They drove on a little while in silence while she thought about this. Then she said, 'So what do I call you? Brother Benedict? Ben? Or just Bro?'

'Benedict will be fine,' he said. Then after a small pause. 'Definitely not Bro.'

'I looked them up on the Internet. Your lot. Bit of a violent history, wouldn't you say?'

'You mean the Crusades.'

'Seems to have gone on a bit longer than that. When the Crusades were well over.'

'There was always a new enemy. But I don't believe we were especially violent. No more than the English – or the Americans.'

He had obviously guessed she was American from her accent, even though it wasn't strong.

'But you were monks. Whatever happened to *Thou Shalt Not Kill*? *Turn the Other Cheek*?'

'We weren't ordinary monks. We were a military order. Our job was to fight the battles of the Church.'

'I see. And now? Still fighting the battles of the Church?'

'We've sheathed the sword,' he said, 'but we keep it handy.'

She glanced sideways at him but he was half turned away from her, gazing out of the side window. Not that there was anything interesting to look at. They passed a sign for the airport.

'So what made you become a monk?' she enquired.

'I was kind of brought up to it.'

'Uh-huh. And is it hard? I mean, d'you have to give up much?'

'Nothing that has struck me as being too great a sacrifice.'

She probed him – gently by her standards – for the rest of the journey. He told her his father had been Austrian but that he'd been brought up and educated in England. No mention of a mother. He had studied theology at Oxford University. He was a Fellow of All Souls College where he still had rooms but he spent most of his life working abroad – for the Order.

'And you knew Kobal?' she said. She remembered his religious title and added 'Brother Boris' with a faint sneer. She still couldn't get her head round it. Kobal – a monk.

'I did. We entered the Order on the same day.'

'So you were quite close?' No response. She tried again. 'What did you make of him?'

'He was a bit odd,' he said.

'*A bit odd?*' She shot him another swift glance. 'Well, I suppose that's one way of putting it.' And now she came to think of it, his psychiatrists hadn't done much better. 'How odd?'

'Well, he had a thing about sin.'

'Don't all monks? Isn't that your thing – sin?'

'It's a point of view,' he conceded. 'But Boris was more into it than most. He thought the human race was so steeped in sin it was doomed. He'd read the signs. Seen the omens.'

'*Omens?*'

'Global conflict, global warming, vanished species, natural disasters . . .'

'Well, it's a point of view,' she echoed. 'The apocalypse. The end of the world.'

'Well, Boris was interested in what comes just before the end of the world.'

She frowned. 'Like what?'

'The rule of Abaddon – the Beast of the Apocalypse.'

'Excuse me?' She couldn't take this seriously. She wondered if Benedict did. She supposed that if it had anything to do with Kobal you had to take it seriously, no matter how mad it seemed.

'The Book of Revelation tells of the coming of seven angels,' he explained. 'They sound seven trumpets. The first four cause widespread destruction. A third of the earth is set on fire, a third of the sea turns to blood, a third of the rivers run dry . . .'

She checked the mirror and pulled into the

outside lane to pass a white van.

'When the fifth angel sounds his trumpet a star falls to earth and opens up the Abyss – the bottomless pit.' He began to quote: '*And from the pit came locusts like horses arrayed for battle. On their heads were crowns of gold; their faces were like human faces, their hair like women's hair, and their teeth like lions' teeth. And they shall have as king over them the angel of the Abyss whose name is Abaddon.*'

'I see.' Another sideways glance. 'You believe all this.'

'We're talking about Kobal.'

'And what's this Abaddon supposed to do when he's about?'

'The received wisdom is that he'll establish a new world order.'

'Like a dictator.'

'Like a dictator.'

'Kobal would like that. So long as it was him.'

'He given everyone a number. They can't buy or sell anything without it. *And it is the number of the Beast which is six hundred and sixty-six.*'

'Six-six-six,' she repeated. 'I've heard of that. The number of the beast. But I didn't know what it meant.' She looked at him again. 'What *does* it mean?'

146

'Don't ask me. It's kept theologians arguing for a long time. But Kobal always had a thing about numbers.'

She shrugged. 'I told you he was mad. Mad, bad and dangerous to know.'

'And I didn't deny it.' A small pause. 'What about this woman we're going to see – is she the same: *mad, bad and dangerous to know*?'

'She was.'

'And yet you let her out?'

'It happens,' she said. 'People are cured. Aren't you lot supposed to believe in redemption?'

He didn't answer. She saw the turn off ahead and pulled into the inside lane. When they came off the motorway she was busy looking for signposts and they drove in silence for a while. She took another turning. The roads grew narrower and there were trees on either side.

'Is this the Royal Forest of Windsor?' He was gazing intently through the side window.

'I don't know,' she shrugged. 'Could be. Windsor Castle isn't far from here.' She glanced at him. 'What is it with you and forests? Or is it another one of Kobal's things?'

'It might be. So she didn't move far away then, this

147

witch, when they let her out?'

'I told you – she came from round here. And she's not a witch. She's given all that up.'

But privately she thought it strange that the woman had chosen to live so close to the hospital when they let her out. She wondered if she'd gone back to the same house she'd lived in before – where she'd murdered her baby. Surely not. She wished now she had found out more about her but it had been difficult enough getting the phone number.

They were approaching a T-junction. 'If you want to be helpful,' she said, 'you can read the directions.'

'Turn right at the T-junction,' he said. 'And then first left.'

They seemed to be in deep countryside already – only minutes after leaving the motorway. A smattering of rain hit the window. She shivered slightly. It would be dark in a couple of hours. She hoped they would be well on their way back to London by then.

They drove several miles down winding country lanes deep into the heart of the forest. The rain grew worse and a violent wind shook the trees bringing twigs and even small branches skittering down on to the road ahead. Emily had no idea where they were or which direction they were heading. Benedict was peering at the scribbled directions as if it was some sort of code. They would have missed the turning if it hadn't been for the cat. It shot across the road, almost under the wheels of the car. Emily slammed on the brakes and swore.

'Sorry,' she muttered to her companion as he pitched forward in his seatbelt.

He pointed to the tumbledown sign half hidden among the wintry undergrowth at the side of the road. *Mistletoe Cottage*. Beside it was a narrow track leading off into the trees.

Emily reversed and turned down it. It was only a little wider than the car and rutted with deep potholes. Ancient oaks rose on either side, their trunks gnarled and twisted into grotesque masks, their upper limbs whipped into frenzied protest by the storm. *Go back, go back*, they seemed to be shrieking. Here and there through the trees they saw what appeared to be a sculptured figure, carved in wood. Others hung from the lower branches, dancing in the wind.

'Did *she* do them?' Benedict wanted to know.

Emily couldn't say. She seemed to recall that the

woman had done some sculpting at Houndwood but she was too busy nursing the Alfa down the track to think about it much. After about five minutes they emerged into a small clearing . . . and there was the cottage. There are cosy cottages and there are not-so-cosy cottages and this was one of the latter: a low white building under a heap of dirty brown thatch with small, dark windows – like eye sockets, Emily thought, in the face of a corpse.

'Mistletoe's a poison,' Benedict remarked. 'Fatal to humans. Did you know that?'

She switched off the engine and they sat there gazing through the rain-lashed windscreen, taking in the details. Not that there was much to take in. The track forked just before the cottage garden and the two branches veered off to either side and disappeared into the forest.

'The place where three tracks meet,' Benedict muttered as if to himself.

Emily shot him a questioning look but he made no further comment. You would have to be mad, she thought, to live in a place like this, especially in the winter. She shivered, even in the warmth of the car, and reached back for her raincoat.

'Come on,' she said, 'let's get it over with.'

They hurried up the garden path, heads bent into the rain. The door remained firmly shut though surely if the woman was there she must have heard the car or seen them through the windows. Emily reached for the iron knocker – there was no bell – but then Benedict seized her arm and pointed up at the roof of the little porch. There, dangling above their heads, was a little star made or straw, like a corn dolly.

'What?' she said, thinking she'd missed something.

'The septagram,' he murmured. 'The seven-pointed star.'

'So?' It was no big deal to have a star hanging outside your door.

But before he could answer they heard the sound of a bolt being drawn – she locks herself in, thought Emily – and the door opened to reveal a large, matronly woman in a blue smock and matching headscarf. She looked nervously at them both, wiping her hands on a large cloth as if she'd been disturbed in the kitchen.

'I'm sorry,' she said. 'I was painting at the back and I didn't hear the car. 'I'm Lindy. Come in, please, out of the rain.'

Emily barely recognized the woman she had last

seen at Houndwood over ten years ago. She had been tall and thin to the point of gauntness with jet-black hair and piercing eyes. Like a large bird, Emily had thought, a wader like a heron or a stork. Now she was more of an owl, blinking in the harsh light of day. Thick spectacles hung on a ribbon round her neck. And the wisps of hair that strayed out from under her headscarf were more grey than black.

Emily introduced herself and her companion, giving him his formal title. The woman could scarcely take her eyes off him. Emily thought she looked frightened. She had been reluctant to meet them at first, when Emily had rung her, but she seemed hospitable enough now.

'Would you like some tea?' she said. 'Or coffee?'

They opted for tea and she went out into the kitchen to put the kettle on.

She had switched the light on when they came in but the room still seemed dark. It was low-ceilinged and timber-beamed, the walls bowing inwards and hung with a few small, nondescript paintings – mostly of trees. Emily felt as if she was *inside* a tree. When they were standing they had to duck their heads and when they sat down it felt like the walls were closing in on them. A fire smouldered in the grate, producing more smoke than flame and very little heat. The only door, other than the one they'd come in by, led off into the kitchen and a flight of wooden stairs led up to the roof, presumably where the bedrooms were. There was no sign of the painting the woman had said she'd been doing.

She emerged from the kitchen, still rubbing her hands anxiously on the cloth.

'I'm not sure I can tell you anything you don't already know,' she said. 'It was so many years ago. It seems to have happened to a different person.'

'I know,' said Emily. Maybe she *was* a different person now. 'But there just might be a small detail here and there . . .'

'I hardly saw the child before it was taken away from me.'

'I know,' said Emily again – and in the same sympathetic tone – though she wasn't too happy about the woman's tone or her choice of words. She couldn't remember her fighting to keep Jade at the time. In fact she'd seemed only too anxious to get rid of her.

'The thing is,' she continued, 'it's more about Dr Kobal than the child . . .'

'Dr Kobal?' The woman frowned as if the name

meant nothing to her. 'What can I tell you about Dr Kobal? I hardly met him. You probably knew him much better than I did.'

'You hardly met him,' said Benedict. It was the first time he had spoken. 'And yet you agreed to carry his child.'

Even in the poor light she seemed to go a little paler. Emily could see the fear in her eyes when they met Benedict's. Fear – and something else she couldn't quite identify.

'He offered me money.' She looked at Emily appealingly. 'I told you at the time. I admitted it.'

Only because they'd checked her bank account and found it there. Emily wondered if they'd let her keep it.

'Fifty thousand down and the rest when the baby was born. Which I never got.'

Benedict leaned forward. 'Did he say what was going to happen to the child when it was born?'

'No.' Again the fear. Her hands were trembling in her lap. She clenched them together. 'I thought he was going to take care of it. He said he'd take care of me, too. Arrange my release. He was a doctor. I trusted him.'

'Why did he choose you?'

She shook her head. 'I don't know. Maybe I was the right age, the right type . . .'

'He'd read your case notes?'

'Yes.' She avoided his eye, looking at Emily instead. 'He knew all about me. It didn't seem to worry him.'

What particular aspect, Emily wondered. The fact that she was a witch? That she thought she was the reincarnation of Morgan-la-Fay – the witch who'd borne King Arthur's baby? The fact that she'd murdered her own?

'And have you seen him since?' she asked. 'Or been in touch with him?'

The woman shook her head violently. 'Not likely,' she said.

'Why did you come back here?' said Benedict suddenly.

'Why shouldn't I? It's my home. Where else would I go?'

So it was true. She had lived here before – before she went to Houndwood. This must be where she'd killed the child. Emily looked up at the stairs and suppressed a shudder.

Benedict was looking around the room and she thought he was thinking the same thing but then he said: 'This is where the circle was, isn't it? The circle of oaks.'

'What do you mean?' She looked imploringly at Emily. Her hands were clenched so tightly the knuckles were white. 'I don't know what he means.'

But nor did Emily.

'Where the Druids worshipped,' he went on. 'Where they sacrificed people.'

She was shaking her head. Her voice was like a little girl's. 'I don't know what you mean.'

'It wasn't just the money, was it?' Benedict's voice was cold, matter-of-fact, like a lawyer's. 'He told you, didn't he, why he chose you to bear his child? She was his Child of the Forest.'

The whistle of the kettle made Emily jump. The woman leaped to her feet.

'The kettle's boiling,' she said. 'I'll go and make tea.'

It should have been funny but nobody laughed.

When she'd left the room Emily looked at Benedict with a frown.

'What did you mean: "She was his Child of the Forest"? Were you talking about Jade?'

'I'm sorry.' He kept his voice low. 'I thought I might shake it out of her.'

He felt in his pocket and pulled out a scrunched-up notebook and a pen. He turned to a blank page and drew seven straight lines in the shape of a star without taking the pen from the page.

'The septagram,' he said. 'Kobal's sign. His signature almost. The seven-pointed star – like the one in the porch. The elven or fairy star, some people call it. Each point has a name.' He ticked them off one by one. 'The four elements: Earth, Fire, Water, Air. And three others: Above, Below and Within. Or, as some would have it: Forest, Sun, Sea, Wind, Moon, Magic, Spirit. Jade is Kobal's Child of the Forest.'

'And there are six more?'

'Yes. So I believe.'

'But – *why*? What did he want with seven children?'

Benedict sighed. 'Seven children from seven different locations. Seven times seven equals . . . six-six-six.'

They sat in silence for a moment. They could hear a branch knocking against a window, whipped by the wind.

'When I went to school,' Emily said, 'seven times seven equalled forty-nine.'

'Not at the school Kobal went to.' Benedict drew

something else on the page and showed it to her. An equation.

$$777 - \frac{777}{7} = 666$$

'But what does it mean?' said Emily.

'I don't know,' he said. 'That's the trouble'

But then he started to quote: '*Let him that hath understanding count the number of the beast: for it is the number of a man; and his number is six hundred threescore and six.* Revelations chapter thirteen verse eighteen.'

'Yes, well, we agreed he was mad.'

'Mad enough to act on it.'

She frowned. It was worrying but she couldn't get her head round it for the moment. Something else was worrying her too. Something closer to hand.

'She's been a long time making tea,' she said.

Benedict was at the door in an instant, his eyes roving the dim interior. Then he crossed to another door at the far end of the kitchen. It opened on to the back garden . . . and the woods.

Emily watched him from the door to the living room.

'What's she up to?' she demanded. She was more puzzled than alarmed.

He dived in his pocket for his mobile phone. Shook his head. 'No signal. Yours?'

Hers was the same.

'Did you phone here?'

'Yes.' She looked for the phone. Saw it at once on the kitchen wall. But he was there before her.

'Dead,' he said.

The word seemed to echo in the empty room.

'How can it . . .?'

'Line's been cut.'

He shut the back door and slid the bolt.

'Out the front,' he said.

They hurried out to the car. She knew before she reached it that there was something wrong. When they got closer she saw what it was. All four tyres had been slashed.

'Who can have . . .?'

She stared at Benedict in dismay. But he was looking past her in the direction of the forest.

There were six of them. They came out of the trees in a rough line and walked purposefully towards them. They wore animal masks and carried long iron bars.

16

The Woodlanders

Emily had a moment of déjà vu. But of course it had happened before. These were the same men – or at least wearing the same masks – who had tried to kidnap Jade.

They were the kind of masks a child might wear for a fancy-dress party. Woodland creatures, more like cartoon animals than the real thing. A squirrel, a fox, a badger . . . even a bunny rabbit. But there was nothing childish about the iron bars they carried or the determined way they advanced towards them as they stood by the disabled car.

'Give me the car keys,' said Benedict softly.

'But . . .' Emily began.

'Please.' He held his hand out but he didn't take

his eyes off the line of men.

She gave him the keys.

'Get in the car.'

She got in the car. This was unusual. She did not usually do what she was told, not without a long and detailed explanation, but the circumstances were exceptional. Benedict got in the driver's side. He started the engine.

'Fasten your seatbelt.'

'But . . .'

She was going to point out that you couldn't drive a car with flat tyres. But he already was.

He slammed the gear into first with a sound that made her wince, gunned the motor and turned the car to face the line of men. Horrible noises came from the slashed tyres. Emily could feel every bump and hollow through the floor. She scrabbled frantically at her seatbelt.

'What are you going . . .'

'To do' came out as a long drawn-out wail, a bit like the wail people give when you reach the top of a rollercoaster and start to go down the other side. Benedict had put his foot down. From the sound the engine made they were still in first or second gear.

The men scattered – all but one, who stood his

ground, holding his iron bar like a spear. He had the face of an owl.

Benedict drove straight for him.

Owl-face hurled the spear.

Benedict's arm shot out and pushed Emily's head down.

There was the sound of a small explosion as the windscreen shattered. The car swerved violently to the left but it was still moving. Emily looked up and caught a glimpse of owl-face through the side window – a moment before Benedict opened the car door and smashed it into him.

He shut the door and spun the wheel. There was an acrid smell of burning rubber. A tyre came off and shot high into the air but he was still turning – or at least sliding. Through the shattered windscreen Emily saw an opening in the line of trees – the track they had taken from the road.

They were heading straight for it when she saw the van. A white van blocking the track a little way into the trees. Benedict braked and slammed the gears into reverse. But they were stuck in the mud.

Through the side window Emily saw the masked figures racing in. She fumbled at her seatbelt so she could get out of the car. At least then she could run.

162

She stood no chance trapped in her seat . . . But then they were moving again. First back, then forward, bouncing and lurching over the rough ground, the engine whining like an animal in pain and the men running before them. One of them turned. The bunny rabbit. He drew back his arm to throw the bar. Emily thought they were going to run him down but at the last moment Benedict spun the wheel and they swung round like a whirligig. Emily's brain felt like it was being hurled round her skull. Before the car had stopped sliding Benedict was out of the door.

She thought he was running away, into the trees. But he was running straight at the man with the iron bar. He seemed to step inside it as it came down, deflecting the blow with his left hand and chopping the edge of the right into the man's neck. The man crumpled in a heap and Benedict ran back to the car.

They chased the men in a wide circle round the clearing. It was like a clown act at the circus. Benedict seemed to be after one in particular – the one in the badger mask. Finally the man made a break for the cottage. He vaulted over the gate and sprinted up the path towards the front door. Benedict didn't even slow down. They hit the gate at about thirty miles an hour and went straight through it – taking a section of fence with them. Emily had ducked down when they hit the gate. When she looked up, badger-man had turned at bay in the porch. For one terrible moment Emily thought they were going to smash straight into him and on through the house. But then Benedict slammed on the brakes.

They smashed into the porch instead. The two wooden uprights crumbled and the porch roof came down. Badger-man disappeared under an avalanche of tile and brick.

Benedict was already reversing.

They backed halfway across the garden. But when he tried to go forward they were stuck fast. The wheel rims were spinning in mud. Smoke rose round the crippled car. Through the side window Emily saw the other men running towards them across the clearing. There were still three of them and they still had their iron bars.

Benedict opened the car door and walked towards them. He met the first in the gap where the fence had been. Emily couldn't make out exactly what he did. He seemed to break step just before they clashed and angle his body sideways. The iron bar sailed through the space where he should have been standing. Then the man shot into the air as if propelled by some invisible force and landed several metres away in a mound of what looked like garden compost. He didn't get up. Benedict kept on walking. The other two men had stopped. A fox and a weasel. They threw their iron bars at the advancing figure. Benedict blocked one with his arm but not the other. Emily clearly saw it strike him high in the head. But he kept on walking. The fox and the weasel looked at each other – then with one accord they ran back towards the woods.

Benedict let them go.

He came back to the car.

'You all right?' he said to Emily.

She nodded. She didn't think she could speak. There was an ugly gash above his right eye and blood was running down the side of his face.

He walked towards the pile of rubble in the porch and dragged out the man in the badger mask. He pulled the mask up and felt his neck for a pulse. Then he let him fall back in the rubble.

Emily found her voice. 'Is he dead?'

Benedict shook his head. 'Just concussed.'

'What about you? You're bleeding.'

He put his hand up to his head and looked at the blood as if in surprise. 'It'll stop,' he said. This didn't seem likely. Blood was pulsing out of the wound. He looked about him. Three more bodies lay scattered around the clearing.

'Are *they* just concussed?' asked Emily.

'I'd better check,' said Benedict. While he was gone she found a scarf at the back of the car to use as a tourniquet but when he came back the wound had stopped bleeding. Just as he'd said it would.

He was looking at the car thoughtfully.

'I don't think this is going anywhere,' he said.

Emily thought he was right. She thought it probably wouldn't go anywhere ever again.

'She must have some form of transport in a place like this,' he said.

He strode off to one of the outbuildings and came back a few moments later wheeling an old motor scooter. A pop-pop.

'Key was on a hook,' he said.

He had a few goes on the kick-starter before he got it working.

'Hop on the back,' he said. 'We'll need a breakdown truck for the car.'

'What about them?' she said, meaning the bodies.

'I'll get some of my people to sort them out,' he said. 'If they're still here.'

Some of my people. Who did he mean – monks? She shook her head in bewilderment.

'You wouldn't think of calling the police?'

'I don't think that would be such a good idea, do you? In the circumstances.'

She looked at the man he'd pulled out of the rubble. Benedict had pulled off his mask and with a shock she realized she'd seen him before. It was the man she'd met outside the Convent of St Mary and St Joseph in Victoria. The homeless man with the dog and an interest in local history.

'Who *are* these people?' she said. 'What do they want with us?'

He shrugged.

'I can only imagine that our witch friend is in touch with Kobal,' he said. 'I didn't think of that. Or I wouldn't have put you in danger.'

'Kobal sent them? To kill us?'

'I rather think he was hoping I would kill one of them,' he said. 'And then I'd have been in real trouble.'

She stared at him. He was probably right.

'Are you really a monk?' she said.

'Yes.' He frowned as if the question puzzled him.

'Come on,' he said. He gunned the throttle. 'Let's get out of here.'

'But . . . shouldn't we question them? They might know where Kobal is. They might even know where Jade is.'

He shook his head. 'No, they won't. They won't even know who we're talking about. Besides, I know where Kobal is. I know where Jade is, too. That's not the problem. It's what he wants with her. And the other kids. That's the problem. Now get on the back. Unless you want to wait for the breakdown truck.'

17

The Dancing Girl
and the Terrible Mother

Jade was back in the clearing in the middle of the forest.

No motorbike this time. And no mysterious figures waiting to guide her. None that she could see anyway.

She looked down each of the tracks in turn. Which one should she choose? They all looked the same.

She closed her eyes, stretched out her arms and began to turn in a circle, faster and faster, like a spinning top until she lost her balance and sat down. She opened her eyes. For a moment it felt as if she was still spinning round. Then things steadied and came into focus and she was looking straight down one of the tracks.

So that was the track she chose.

She set off with some confidence, compared to the last time she had played the game. She wasn't here, not really, not physically. She was an avatar. An incarnation, like a goddess descended into the realm of mere mortals . . .

Then she remembered what Kobal had said when she asked him if she could have been killed – like Rodrigo. *I guess so*. Faintly surprised, as if the thought had just occurred to him.

Great, she thought.

She stopped and looked back but she could no longer see the clearing at the end of the track; it seemed to be lost in a kind of haze or mist. She had a sense that night was falling, back there at any rate. She looked up at the sky and was surprised to see it was a bright, almost painful blue. Then, just above the height of the trees she saw a balloon – no, not a balloon – a kite. It drifted lazily into view and away over the trees. A simple red kite shaped like a triangle with a length of string hanging down, as if it had snapped or someone had let go of it. Which meant that someone had once been holding it. Possibly not very far away.

She watched it out of sight. Then set off resolutely

down the path in the same direction.

She had been walking for some time without any of the usual tricks. No blinding lights, no strange figures through the trees. But then she noticed that the trees were different: tropical, like the trees in Kobal's sunroom. And there was lush vegetation growing among them and the air was filled with birdsong. Exotic birdsong.

But of course, she was in India.

India!

She instantly thought of tigers, even though she knew India had changed a great deal since the time of *The Jungle Book* and there weren't many tigers left. But if Kobal had anything to do with it there would be tigers. She peered cautiously through the trees.

No tigers. But there *was* something.

A figure, squatting in the middle of the path a little way ahead of her. At first she thought it was a monkey but as she drew closer she saw it was a child. A little girl with long dark hair and a simple brown dress. And she was crying. Sobbing her heart out.

'Excuse me,' said Jade hesitantly, 'have you lost your mummy?'

She didn't know why she said this. Only later,

when she knew the truth, did she realize how amazing it was.

The child looked up at her through her tears and pointed up at the nearest tree – and there, caught up in the branches about halfway up, was the red kite.

'Oh, you've lost your kite,' said Jade rather foolishly (she was feeling rather foolish as a matter of fact).

The child nodded.

'Would you like me to get it down for you?'

Another nod – and the trace of a smile. She was a very beautiful little girl and there was something vaguely familiar about her.

Jade approached the tree. She was quite good at climbing trees and this one didn't look especially difficult. The branches came down quite low and there was a thick rope of ivy or some such coiled around one of them, just within jumping distance. Jade jumped – but as soon as her fingers closed around it she realized she had made a terrible mistake. It wasn't ivy or any other kind of parasite. It was a snake.

Jade gave a cry and feel sprawling to the ground. Before she could get up the snake had dropped off the branch and coiled itself around her. Its narrow pointed head was raised above her and she was staring into a pair of black, snake-like eyes.

Jade tried to remember if she'd made any notes in her survivor's guidebook about what to do when confronted by snakes. She rather thought that the chief piece of advice had been not to go near one. And if you absolutely couldn't avoid it you had to trap its head in a forked stick.

This did not seem very practical. In the first place she did not have a forked stick. In the second the head in question looked rather too large to fit into anything smaller than a fork-lift truck.

Then it opened its mouth and she nearly fainted.

She could see right down its throat.

The main features of which were its black flickering tongue and a pair of sharp pointed fangs.

Then it spoke.

'Welcome,' it hissed. 'My name is Death.'

Jade was aware that in real life a snake could not speak. Therefore this could not be real life. It was the game. This was only slightly reassuring. Kobal had not been too clear about the rules concerning Death. And if there *were* any rules, clearly the snake had not read them.

Its head came closer. Its jaws opened wider.

Then a small voice said, 'Stop that!'

Jade dragged her eyes away from the snake's and looked up.

The little girl was standing above them with her hands on her hips and a look of cold fury on her face. She stamped her foot on the ground.

'Stop that at once!' she said.

For a moment Jade wondered if she meant her.

'Me?' she began indignantly. But then she looked at the snake. It had closed its mouth. It may even have gulped. There was a new look in its eyes. Jade was not practised at reading a snake's eyes but if she had been asked to describe the look in a single word it would have been *sheepish*. She felt its coils sliding off her. Then it wriggled off into the undergrowth.

Jade stood up. She looked at the child with awe. 'Thank you,' she gasped.

The child seemed entirely unconcerned. At least about the snake. But she pointed up at the tree again to where the kite still dangled halfway up.

'OK, OK, I'll get your kite,' Jade assured her hastily. A child who could do that to snakes was clearly not a child to be mucked about with.

This time she was more careful where she put her hands, but in a very short time she had swarmed up to where the kite, was and she was lifting it up very carefully so it didn't catch on a twig and rip – when she saw the house.

If it *was* a house.

It was a little further along the path, in a clearing among the trees. A large white building with several layers, a bit like a wedding cake.

And then she saw the people.

They were on a kind of terrace immediately in front of the building. Four men and a woman.

Two of the men were playing musical instruments – a flute and a kind of guitar – and the woman was dancing. The other two men were watching. One of them was tall and bearded, stripped to the waist but with a yellow turban on his head. He just stood there with his arms folded. The other man was smaller and he had a backpack and a stick which he was leaning on with both hands, his head nodding away to the music, staring at the woman.

Jade could see why.

She wore a long, flowing robe in some delicate material that rose about her in a gorgeous gossamer cloud of cinnamon and red and yellow, and she had long black hair that whipped from side to side as she danced. Even at this distance Jade could see that she was very beautiful, like some fabulous fluttering butterfly.

Jade had read about the famous Indian dancing girls. This must be one of them.

The music grew wilder and wilder and the dancing girl danced faster and faster and Jade felt dizzy just watching her. Then she was distracted by a movement in the tree just beneath her and she looked down in sudden panic, fearful that it was the snake, or one of its fellows. But it was the little girl. Either from impatience or curiosity she had followed Jade up the tree and she was clinging to the branches with a determined expression on her face. Jade was about to warn her to be careful when she saw her expression change. She was staring towards the building and with a look of such horror that Jade turned swiftly back to see what was the matter.

The two musicians were still playing. The woman was still dancing. The backpacker was still watching as if entranced. But the other man had unwound the yellow turban from his head and as Jade watched, too horrified to scream or shout a warning, he looped it round the other man's neck from behind and pulled it tight.

The backpacker kicked and struggled and clawed at the yellow material wound round his throat and the strangler stood behind him with his feet braced wide apart and the muscles standing out in his arms as he pulled it tighter and tighter. It was like a kind of dance in itself. In fact, the woman and the musicians carried on as if it was all part of the performance.

Then, just as the music reached a climax, the backpacker stopped struggling and went limp. And the other man let go of one end of the yellow scarf and stepped back, sliding it almost ceremoniously from his victim's neck as the man slumped to the ground.

The music stopped. And the dancer collapsed, as if exhausted by her performance. Or it might have been a curtsy.

Jade looked down toward the little girl to express her horror and amazement at what they had just seen. But the little girl wasn't there. Nor was the kite. Jade looked back towards the group of people on the terrace. But they weren't there either. It was as if she had imagined the whole thing.

But the building was still there.

Jade climbed shakily down from the tree. This was just a game, she reminded herself. Nothing in it was real. All she could do was go on until Kobal decided that either he or she had had enough and brought her back to reality, or at least his version of it. The important thing was to find the little girl again because Jade had a pretty good idea that she was one of Kobal's missing children.

So on she went, following the path through the forest – and almost immediately she came to the white building. The path went right up to the front door, which had been left slightly open.

Now what should she do?

She looked back. The path was still there. She could go back the way she had come. But it seemed rather tame.

Taking a deep breath, Jade stepped through the door . . .

And found herself in a large empty room rather like an old-fashioned dance hall, filled with a thin haze of smoke and with shafts of sunlight pouring in through two rows of small ornate arches high up on the walls. The effect was as if the building had been pierced by dozens of crossed swords or lances made of sunlight.

Then she saw the figure standing against the far wall.

She drew back in alarm thinking it was the dancing girl – dancing in a circle of blazing candles.

But she was so still. As if frozen in the middle of a

dance step with one leg raised almost to her waist and bent at the knee.

And she had four arms.

It was a statue.

But what a statue.

As Jade approached she began to make out the gruesome details through the smoke.

One hand was holding a sword and another was holding a man's head – cut off at the neck.

The other two hands were empty and were raised palms outward as if stopping traffic.

But she was probably not a policewoman, Jade decided.

For one thing she was stark naked apart from a belt round her waist – a belt composed of human heads and severed arms. Also she was sticking her tongue out in a most disgusting fashion. And she was dancing on a dead body.

Jade stared, wondering what to make of her.

'Her name is Kali,' said a voice – and Jade practically jumped out of her skin. She whipped round and there, standing just behind her, was the hooded figure of a monk.

At first she thought it was Kobal, for it wore the same black robe and cowl that she had seen him wearing in the Castle of Demons.

She tried to make out his features through the smoke.

But he didn't have a face.

Either that or it was in deep shadow.

She drew back, really frightened now.

'Who are you?' Her voice came out like a thin croak.

'Kali,' repeated the man. But he wasn't talking about himself. He raised his hand towards the dancing statue. 'The Hindu goddess of life and death. This is one of her incarnations. You could call it an avatar. Dakshina Kali. The Gentle One. The Earth Mother. Giver of life.'

Jade looked back at the statue. If this was the gentle one what were the others like?

Almost as if he knew what she was thinking, the monk went on: 'Beware the Smashan Kali, the Terrible Mother, Bringer of Death and Destruction.'

And right on cue the door opened and the man in the yellow turban came in.

Jade drew back into the circle of smoke and flame around the statue. And then she felt something like a draught on the back of her neck. She turned again and saw a bright light behind the figure, so bright it almost dazzled her.

Taking a deep breath, as if she was about to dive into a pool, she ducked under the raised leg of the goddess, and jumped.

At once she was in the open air.

She was standing on the far side of the building. There was another terrace and steps leading down to a river. And on the bank of the river a great crowd of people gathered around a kind of platform stacked high with logs.

And on top of the platform was a dead body.

Jade stepped back, clapping her hand to her mouth to stifle a scream.

Was this the man she had just seen strangled to death?

And now she could see the dancing girl and the two musicians among the crowd on the river bank . . . And they were looking up towards her.

She drew back into the smoke and the shadows at the side of the building and just as she did the man in the yellow turban emerged.

He was wearing a long robe now, also yellow, and carrying a flaming torch. He didn't seem to notice Jade but went straight down the steps towards the river and the crowd parted before him, everyone bowing and making a kind of salute with their hands to their foreheads. He went straight up to the platform with the dead body and put the torch to the logs, which immediately burst into flame.

Jade seized her chance to sneak back into the temple but her escape route was blocked by the figure of Kali.

She had turned round – it was impossible but she had – and she looked different. Her tongue wasn't sticking out but her eyes burned with a fierce red light.

And then a voice, as if from inside her own head, said, 'Beware the Smashan Kali, the Terrible Mother, goddess of Death and Destruction.'

Then she heard a shout behind her and she whirled round to see the man in the yellow turban framed by the fiery furnace pointing straight at her.

There was only one way to go. Back into the building. But the Kali wouldn't let her.

Whichever way Jade tried to go there was an arm or a leg stopping her. She felt a terrible panic as if she was drowning . . .

And then she felt the scarf around her neck.

18

In the Forest

'*You know where she is?*'

Emily stared at Benedict in astonishment. 'But you said you had no idea . . .'

'Kind of,' he said — but distantly, as if he was thinking of something else. 'Now get on the back.'

He put the bike into gear and she jumped on before he drove off without her. She clung to him as they bounced over the roots of the trees and skirted the puddles in the muddy track. She could see the tyre tracks of the white van in the soft ground ahead of them. But she had something far more important on her mind.

'So where is she?' she yelled in Benedict's ear. She was ready to beat it out of him, even after what she had seen him do to the men in the animal masks.

He said something but she couldn't quite hear. It sounded like: 'Searching for her . . .'

'Well – we're all searching for her,' she yelled, furious now . . . 'But you said you *knew*.'

Then suddenly he braked.

She nearly fell off into one of the puddles.

'What is it?' she cried out in alarm.

She stood up in the seat and peered over his shoulder, half expecting to see more of the men waiting in ambush for them down the track. But the track was empty.

'Shush,' said Benedict. He had turned his head as if he was listening for something.

Emily listened too. But she could hear nothing. Just the dripping of the rain in the trees.

'What is it?' she said again.

But he raised a hand to silence her.

Then he closed his eyes as if he was concentrating or in pain.

19

Tiger!

Jade couldn't breathe. She tried to claw the scarf away from her throat but it was too tight. She couldn't get her fingers into it. She tried to reach behind her head to claw at the man's face but she couldn't do that either.

He was too strong and her own strength was fading.

She tried to use her powers, to read what was in his mind. But all he had in his mind was her death. And her own fear was too great for her to concentrate on anything else.

Ahead of her through the smoke and the ashes she could see the figure of Kali. The Smashan Kali, the Terrible Mother: Her eyes seemed to bore into Jade's skull.

So now she knew what it felt like to die.

She wondered if Kobal could feel it, too. Surely he wouldn't let this happen to her. In his game. She would wake up as if out of a terrible nightmare. Or he would come and rescue her like the last time, on his motorbike.

She could feel her eyes clouding over.

Was it possible to die in cyberspace?

And if you did, what would become of you – the *real* you?

And then through the smoke and flames came a figure, and it wasn't Kali. It was the cowled figure of the monk.

Jade could barely make him out. It was as if he was part of the smoke. But he was speaking to her. Or at least she could hear the voice in her head.

'Do as I do,' he was saying. 'Be what I am.'

Then the figure, or the smoke, seemed to envelop her and she felt an enormous strength flow through her limbs.

And she knew what she had to do.

She raised her right leg high like the dancer in the temple . . . And then she brought it down with all the new-found power that was inside her, smashing her heel into the man's instep.

The scream was like an animal's when the trap springs shut.

Jade was already turning, grinding her heel deep into the exact angle where the leg meets the foot. She could almost feel the bones crunching.

The scarf was still tight around her neck but there was a space between their two bodies and into this space she drove her elbow, as hard and as viciously as she could.

The scream died in the man's throat and became a woof of exploding air.

Jade was still turning, with more room now for manoeuvre. The man was doubled up, still clinging to the scarf but his face a mask of shock and pain. She brought her right arm up sharply between then, smashing the heel of her palm into the angle of his jaw, just below the left ear.

She felt something give . . . Another animal cry and the man let go of the scarf and fell back with a hand to the side of his face.

And Jade knew, with the new knowledge she had, that she had dislocated his jaw.

He fell back down the steps.

Jade pulled the scarf from her throat.

There were more men running up the steps

towards her.

Now what? thought Jade. She was ready to take them all on.

But the voice in her head thought otherwise. 'Run, you fool,' it said.

The Kali was still there; her eyes glowed like burning coals through the smoke and ashes. Her sword arm was raised. A flash of light caught the blade as it swung down through the air.

Jade jumped.

Through the smoke-filled gap under the Smashan's leg . . .

And back into the building.

Except that it wasn't the same building.

It was filled with light – and sound. And people.

They sat in a great circle all around her – hundreds of people in seats rising in tiers like in a theatre or a stadium. And Jade seemed to be on a kind of stage. A circular stage – with bars dividing her from the audience. Like an exhibit in a cage.

She turned around to look back the way she had come.

Behind her was the circle she had just jumped through.

But that wasn't the same either.

It was a circle of flame – but there was no Kali, neither the Gentle One nor the Terrible Mother.

Just a tiger . . .

Of course. You could always count on Kobal.

It leaped straight through the middle of the circle of flame and landed almost on top of her.

'Ooooh,' screamed the crowd.

Jade watched – almost paralysed with fear – as the tiger bounded off to the right. Why hadn't it killed her?

Then she saw the girl.

She stood in centre stage, just behind Jade, dressed all in red – tight red top, red baggy trousers and a red turban, all sparkling with golden stars. And she carried a long whip.

She looked even more startled than Jade was. But she was quicker to pull herself together.

'Behind me,' she said, making a quick gesture with her arm. Then she whirled round to face the tiger, cracking her whip.

Jade scuttled behind her and peered over her shoulder.

The tiger snarled and crouched as if ready to spring. Then, almost on its belly, it moved in a circle around them. But it kept its distance.

The girl shouted at it in a language Jade did not understand. Then she turned to face the circle of flame and cracked her whip again.

Something moved in the smoke.

Then another tiger jumped through the hoop.

'Ooooh,' cried the crowd.

'Ohhhhh,' moaned Jade.

She knew where she was now – even if she didn't have the faintest idea how she had got here.

She was in the middle of a circus ring.

And there was no way out except through the flaming hoop.

Crack went the whip and the second tiger followed the first around the edge of the ring.

Another crack of the whip. Another tiger jumped through the hoop.

Again and again until there were seven full-grown tigers slinking around the edge of the circle, snarling and glaring at the girl in red – and the other girl who crouched in terror behind her.

Jade didn't know if the tigers could see her.

She didn't know if the audience could see her – but she wasn't so worried about them.

The girl kept moving in a circle, trying to keep her eyes on all the tigers at once, and Jade moved with her, sticking as close behind her as possible.

The girl clearly had some kind of power over them – and it wasn't just because she carried a whip. It was something more than that. It was as if she had hypnotized them.

Then Jade remembered the girl in the forest who had saved her from the snake.

Could this be the same girl?

She was older, almost as old as Jade, but there was something of the same confidence – and authority – about her.

And wow, how she put those tigers through it!

They moved backwards and forwards as if they were dancing; they rose on their hind legs, clawing at the air like pussy cats. They purred as if they were singing.

There was music, too. Western music. A song Jade knew.

And the tigers sang and danced.

But they were so angry.

Jade could sense their anger, she could see it in their eyes. But they didn't seem to be able to help themselves. They seemed to be in thrall to the girl in red.

But not entirely. Jade sensed that a single slip on

the girl's part, a single lapse in concentration, and they would tear her apart.

And Jade, too, if her experience on the dump was anything to go by.

Finally the girl let them go. She shouted a string of commands and cracked her whip and one by one they all jumped back through the hoop.

The girl bowed in all four directions, with Jade still moving behind her. The crowd clapped and cheered. Then she grabbed Jade's hand and they ran towards the ring of fire and jumped together.

'What did you think you were *doing*?' demanded the girl.

She seemed to be quite angry.

She tore off her red-and-gold turban and her long black hair came tumbling down almost as far as her waist. Now Jade was reminded of the dancing girl.

'I don't know,' she said. She looked about her.

They were still in the circus tent, somewhere backstage. Or whatever the back of a circus was called. There were lots of people about – circus people: clowns, men on stilts, a dwarf, a woman with huge muscles in a leopard skin, but no one seemed to be taking any notice of them. There was straw on the floor and a strong smell of animals but no sign of the tigers.

The girl seized Jade by the arm again and pulled her through a gap in the side of the tent. They stepped over the guy ropes and Jade blinked in harsh sunlight.

They were in a large field full of caravans and cars and cages.

'How did you get into my circus ring?' demanded the girl. 'You nearly got us both killed.'

She spoke good English – but then so had Paco in the tip. Perhaps it was something to do with the game.

Jade raised her arms helplessly. 'I just jumped through the hoop,' she said. 'And there I was.'

As explanations went, this wasn't one of Jade's better efforts. She could tell the girl wasn't impressed.

'So how did *you* get here?' asked Jade with what was meant to be a disarming smile.

But then she saw that the girl was staring past her towards the circus tent and her eyes were filled with fear.

What could scare a girl like this?

Jade turned. And saw a man watching them from the side of the tent. A man in a yellow turban.

'Not again,' said Jade.

And now other men were coming out of the tent.

'Go,' said the girl urgently. 'Go now. Hurry.'

'Come with me,' Jade insisted, reaching out for her.

But the girl pushed her away.

'Run,' she said. 'Before it's too late.'

The men were starting to move towards them.

'I'll come back for you,' said Jade. 'I'll tell Kobal. He'll send people for you.'

'Run,' the girl almost screamed.

Jade turned and ran.

But where could she run to?

The field of caravans and cages seemed to go on for ever . . . And the men were coming after her. Animals roared at her from their cages. Monkeys shrieked and rattled their bars. She glimpsed the tigers again – pacing and glaring furiously. She ducked under a line of washing, dodged around a pen with some pigs in it, round the side of a caravan . . . and almost into a cage of wolves.

They leaped at the bars in a frenzy of saliva and snarling teeth.

Jade sprang back and looked around her in a panic . . . She seemed to be surrounded by trailers and cages full of animals and birds, roaring and screeching at her.

Then she saw the red kite.

It came drifting down, slowly over the roofs of the caravans, with its long tail trailing beneath it. Down, down . . . until it was almost hovering above her head.

The men came hurtling round the side of the nearest caravan. They skidded to a halt when they saw her. Then with a roar they charged.

Jade reached up and seized the tail of the kite.

It was ridiculous but it was all she had.

And at once she felt a violent tug in her arms. She was jerked off her feet. She rose like a helium balloon. Up, up and away, over the roofs of the caravans, over the top of the circus tent, way up high into the burnished brass sky . . .

And then Kobal was lifting the helmet up off her head and pulling the electrodes away from her temples and she was back in his study in Castle Piru.

20

The Child of Magic

'The girl from the circus, she's one of us, isn't she?'

Jade was feeling cocky. Not only had she survived another session of the game but she'd found another one of the missing children. At least she thought she had.

Kobal nodded in confirmation. But he didn't seem too pleased about it – or with Jade. He was frowning over the desktop, moving the mouse about and clicking away like mad, as if he was searching for something.

'What's up?' she asked him. 'Was I supposed to bring her back with me or something? Only there wasn't much room on the kite.'

As usual her sarcasm was lost on Kobal.

'That's all right,' he said absently. 'I'll send some of

my people for her, now I know where she is.'

'Don't mention it. No trouble at all. Apart from a few tigers, the Mad Strangler of Mujirama and the Goddess of Death and Destruction. Next time you lose another kid just give me a shout.'

He looked at her then with faintly arched brows. 'Aren't you forgetting someone?'

She considered. 'Oh yes, the snake. And probably the odd psycho hiding in the bushes. To tell the truth I was moving so fast I didn't notice. Did you see me?' She slid off the chair and demonstrated a few karate chops. '*Bam! Kerblam! Splat!*'

'Quite,' he murmured dryly. 'Quite the little Catwoman. You and Baer-Mellor must have been busy in the gym.'

Something in his tone and the look he gave her warned her she was on dangerous ground, but what was new about that?

'So who else managed to attract your attention?' he enquired with deadly politeness. 'Let me give you a clue? Long black robe. Hood. *Bam, kerblam, splat.*'

'Oh, the monk.'

'Oh, the monk.'

'Wasn't that you?'

'No, it was not me. As I think you know very well.'

'Then who was it?'

'You tell me.'

'*I* don't know. Why should *I* know?'

'Because, my dear, you brought him into the game. From some peculiar part of your brain that I clearly haven't got to know as well as I ought.'

He stared hard at her and she shivered. It was like he was *reading* her. Scrolling through the information stored on a computer.

'I don't know who he was,' she muttered. 'I don't know who any of them were.' She felt drained all of a sudden. 'Or where they came from or anything.'

He continued to study her for a moment. Then he said, 'Well, let me enlighten you. The girl is called Shrika and she is my little Child of Magic. Her mother was a student of mine at the School of Magic in Kerala.'

'You *taught* – at a School of *Magic*?'

Though why that should surprise her she had no idea.

'They have them all over India. Some are better than others. They teach the usual tricks of the trade. Snake-charming, the Indian rope trick, walking on hot coals, lying on a bed of nails. Classic fakir stuff. Still, Shrika's mother had a talent for it and Shrika . . . well, Shrika is something special. As you might expect.'

Jade pondered this information for a moment. There were so many questions she wanted to ask it was hard to know where to begin.

'So . . . who was her mother? I mean, in the game?'

'Can't you guess?'

'The dancing girl?'

'Right. The dancing girl. Or *naatch* girl, as we call them in India. Atima. Lovely girl but a bit of an airhead, as we used to say. Which is doubtless why she went off with the dreaded Sayed.'

'The who?'

'The man in the yellow turban. The *jamaadar*. The leader of a band of Thugs. I must say that was a surprise. I thought that was a thing of the past but apparently not.' He noted her blank expression and explained patiently, 'The Thugs are a religious cult dedicated to the worship of Kali. Their particular speciality is, or was, waylaying travellers and strangling them as a religious sacrifice – after first robbing them of all their belongings. Neatly combining worship and profit, like many another religion.'

'Is that allowed?'

'No, it is not allowed.' He rolled his eyes. 'Sometimes, my dear, I wonder if I made a mistake with you. I didn't know it was still practised but it appears that Sayed decided it was a suitable career for a budding psycho, as you would doubtless describe him. Atima was the bait. I might have known she'd get in with the wrong crowd. She was always attracted to psychos.'

Like you, you mean, Jade thought but wisely didn't say. It was dangerous enough to think it – but he probably wasn't concentrating.

'Yes, I think we do have certain things in common,' Kobal murmured smoothly. 'But Sayed isn't as gifted as I am. The police were on to him so he gave up being a Thug and went into the circus business. Kidnapping clever little girls like Shrika and making them jump through hoops – or in her case, making tigers jump through hoops. No wonder I couldn't find her.'

'But you have now,' said Jade. Thanks to me, she added silently, hoping he would pick it up.

He gazed at her thoughtfully. 'Yes, thanks to you. We can only hope her experience of Thuggery and the Indian circus hasn't entirely spoiled her for our own more worthy endeavours.'

'I don't think she had anything to do with the murders. She seemed as shocked as I was.'

'Yes. She did, didn't she? Well, once we've got her

away from Sayed and that terrible mother of hers perhaps we can do something about bringing out her real talents.'

'Which are?'

'Never mind that. It's *your* special talents I want to talk about. I want to know where you got the idea of the monk from?'

'*My* idea? How could he be *my* idea? I thought you sent him to get me away from the Thugs.'

'Well, I didn't. And believe me, he's a lot more dangerous than Sayed and his little playmates.'

'So you do know who he was?'

He studied her in that careful way he had sometimes, usually when he was coming to some kind of a conclusion. Then he said, 'There isn't anything you can hide from me, Jade, you know that, don't you?'

She flushed. 'I'm not hiding anything from you.'

'No? Well, let's leave it there for the moment.'

But she didn't want to leave it there.

'So who *was* he then?' She stared at him defiantly.

'It's enough for you to know that he's the Enemy. And not to be trifled with.'

The Enemy. Kobal had given her repeated warnings about the people he called the Enemy but he had never explained who or what he meant. Sometimes he seemed to mean the men in the forest who were watching the castle – the *Sami* reindeer herders and hunters. Sometimes the people who had locked him up in Houndwood: people like her Aunt Em and other scientists who he said were jealous of his talents. Other times he seemed to mean the Catholic Church – or some mysterious branch of it.

But of course. The monk . . .

'The less you know about him the better,' Kobal said firmly. 'You don't want him in your brain. I don't know how he got there in the first place – but I may have to give you something to keep him out.'

She didn't like the sound of that.

He peered at the computer screen again as if he might find him there. But then with a sigh he gave the mouse a final click and swung around in his swivel chair.

'OK,' he said in a different, more businesslike tone. 'Let's go.'

'Let's go where?' She'd only just got back.

'Not far. I've got a surprise for you.'

Oh no, she thought. Her father's surprises had a way of turning out to be extremely unpleasant – and frequently life-threatening.

21

The Surprise

Jade's surprise was waiting for her in the sunroom. He was a lot cleaner than the last time she'd seen him but she knew him at once.

The Artful Dodger of Rubbish Dump Number Three. *El Jefe*, the chief of the *chicos*.

Paco.

With his feet up by the pool and a can of Coke in his hand.

'Our little *chico* chicken,' said Kobal. 'Back in the family coop.'

'Hi,' Jade said a little breathlessly. Kobal had said he'd have him here before the week was out but it was still a bit of a shock. She supposed she should be pleased to see him – after all the trouble she'd taken to find him — but she couldn't help feeling a mite cautious. She hadn't known Paco long but it was long enough to know he had a mean streak as wide as the smile on the face of a tiger.

Some little chicken. He still had that shock of wiry black hair and the look of a cunning old goblin.

'*Hola*,' he said, waving the can at her. But he didn't smile and his eyes measured her shrewdly.

'Paco knows all about the game,' said Kobal. 'He's been looking forward to meeting you in the flesh. Right, Paco?'

Paco grunted unconvincingly and took another sip at his Coke.

Jade wondered if he saw her as a potential threat: an obstacle to be negotiated — or removed — like everybody else he'd ever met in his short life.

But he *was* her little brother after all. Her half-brother, anyway. And he'd had a tough time of it. It was up to her to make him feel at home. Among family and friends.

Perhaps she should offer to show him around.

'Paco's already had a squint round the old dump,' Kobal assured her. 'He seems pretty impressed, eh, *chico*?'

Jade supposed anything would be an improvement

on Rubbish Dump Number Three – even the Castle of Demons.

'Never seen snow before, had you, Paco?'

Paco shook his head but somehow Jade didn't think he'd be out in the courtyard making a snowman.

'Soon as he's settled in, Paco's going to be helping you find the rest of the brood,' Kobal told her.

Another little surprise.

'You mean – together?'

She wondered how that would work. He hadn't been much help to her in the dump.

But Kobal didn't mean together.

'I thought we might have a little competition,' he said. 'Like hide and seek. See who can find our next little chicken. Talking of which – how about lunch? Paco?'

Paco's eyes lit up and Jade's heart went out to him. Poor little guy. All those years scrounging for scraps on the tip. She remembered the first time she'd seen him, picking at a pizza he'd found in the rubbish.

'Right on,' said Kobal. 'I think we'll eat by the pool.'

He clapped his hands and Laurie shambled up from wherever he had been lurking among the greenery.

It seemed a long time since Jade had seen the bear and she realized she'd missed him. He was the only real friend she had in the castle. She gave him a big smile but he was looking at Kobal in that nervous way he had.

'I think we'll start with a little soup. Cold soup. You ever tried vichyssoise, Paco? You'll love it.'

Paco looked a little bemused, as well he might. Jade had no idea what vichyssoise was when it was at home but she was pretty damn sure it wasn't on the menu at Rubbish Dump Number Three, Guatemala City.

Welcome to the madhouse, she thought.

'Excellent.' Kobal clapped his hands and rubbed them together. 'And then I think one of Cook's special chicken salads followed by a summer pudding with fruits of the forest. And a bottle of Crémant. The rosé, I think. A little light lunch. Right, Lours? Good man.'

The bear shuffled off. How could it understand him? And how could it make the cook understand? Unless the cook was another bear. Jade had never been in the kitchen. Even after two months there were parts of the castle that were a complete mystery to her.

She snuck a glance at Paco to see how he was coping with the mysteries of Castle Piru. But he seemed perfectly at ease. Maybe after contending with the vultures and the dogs and the rats on the rubbish dump he could take a bear or two in his stride. Even a bear like Laurie who could bring you a dish of cold soup.

'Now thanks to Jade's heroic efforts in India we have only four of the family left to find,' said Kobal with the suggestion of a sneer about the word *heroic*. 'But where are they hiding? That's what we want to know.'

He fingered the seven-pointed star hanging round his neck and his eyes took on a dreamy look.

'What's that rhyme? The one you sing when you see magpies. Jade, you must know it.'

'One for sorrow, two for joy,' she began. 'Three for a girl, four for a boy . . .'

But then her eyes filled with tears for it was a rhyme her godmother, Aunt Em, used to sing to her when she was little. She turned her head away so neither of them would see, but she had a feeling that Kobal already had.

'Five for silver, six for gold, seven for a secret never to be told,' he finished for her. 'Don't suppose they taught you that on the tip, eh, Paco? Not the best place for magpies – I expect the vultures scare the pants off them. I knew Jade would know it, though. Brings back happy memories of her childhood. She has happy memories, you know, unlike some of us. Now where did I put them?'

Jade looked at him sharply because he sounded just like her other father – her *foster* father – when he couldn't find his glasses.

But Kobal didn't mean his glasses. He meant his children.

'I know where they're *meant* to be but you just can't rely on people these days, can you? "Stay there until I come for you," I said. But do they take any damn notice? Do they heck. Paco, look at you, wandering all over South America getting up to all manner of mischief. Even Jade here tried to hide from me. But we'll find them. Even if we have to go seven ways to Hell and back.'

He fingered the star again, turning it round between finger and thumb, pressing the points into his flesh so that even from where she sat Jade could see the marks they made.

'We have found the Child of Magic – thanks to Jade.' With a little mocking bow. 'So that just leaves four. Two girls and two boys. The Child of the Wind and the Child of the Sea,' he crooned. 'The Child of the Moon and the Child of the Spirit.'

What was he on about?

Jade snatched another glance at Paco to see if he knew. It was hard to tell.

'So what are *we*?' she asked, greatly daring. 'Me and Paco?'

Kobal smiled. 'Can't you guess? What's like Wind and Sea but isn't either?'

She groaned inwardly. She hated riddles.

'Or to put it another way – Air and Water,' he prompted her.

Air and Water. They were elements. And the other two were . . .

'Fire and Earth,' she said.

'Fire and Earth. There's a clever girl. Would you have known that, Paco? Course you would. Fire and Earth. So who's Fire and who's Earth?'

Well, Paco was clearly Fire. He looked like he was nursing it inside him, like the fire of the volcano, keeping it burning, waiting for a time when he could use it.

Which made her Earth. Rather depressingly. A plodder.

'I think of you as my Child of the Forest,' said Kobal, 'if that makes you feel any better.'

Out of the corner of her eye she spotted Laurie coming back with a tray. It contained a large soup tureen and a stack of bowls and he was moving very slowly with his eyes fixed on them as if daring them to slide about. She knew how difficult it was for Laurie to carry things and she willed him to reach them without any accidents.

She saw that Kobal was watching him, too, and she had a feeling he was willing something quite different.

'Come on, Lours,' he shouted suddenly. 'You can do it!'

It was a delicate moment. The bear had almost reached the table. But the sudden shout distracted him. The tray teetered in his hands. The big bowl of soup started to slide. He made a desperate attempt to save the situation but only made it worse. Over he went. The soup shot high into the air and came down on his head.

The soup was green and there was a lot of it.

He sat there with the bowl upside down on top of his head and what looked like green slime dripping down all over his face and neck and shoulders. He looked very sorry for himself.

'Waiter, waiter,' Kobal cried, 'there's a bear in my soup.'

He thought this was so funny. He threw himself back in his chair, holding his stomach with both hands and kicking his legs in the air.

Jade watched him in amazement. He was such a child. She knew, of course, that this had been the whole purpose of the exercise, just so he could come up with that pathetic line.

She saw Paco looking at Kobal and thought he looked disgusted too. But it wasn't disgust; it was something else. Something like curiosity. Then he looked at the bear and creased up. *Ho, ho, ho,* he went, and said something in Spanish and he and Kobal were practically wetting themselves.

She went over to Laurie and tried to wipe him down with a pile of napkins but it was hopeless, his fur was full of cold green soup.

'Go have a bath,' she said. She pointed. 'In the pool.'

'Don't even think about it,' said Kobal, wiping his eyes. 'Off to the yard. Roll around in the snow. Oh my.' He sat up in his chair and poured himself some water. 'Oh my, a laugh like that takes years off your life.' He saw the way Jade was looking at him. 'What's the problem?'

'You're the problem,' she said. 'You're just a big kid.'

'Well, at least now I've got another guy to play with.' He threw his arm around Paco, who sat there with a satisfied smirk on his face. 'A guy with a decent sense of humour.'

Jade bit her tongue so she wouldn't say something she might regret.

And deep in her heart she felt a pang of jealousy.

It was the way Kobal had his arm flung round Paco, like they were best buddies. He never did that to her. She didn't think she wanted him to, but . . .

Somewhere, deep down, she knew she wanted his approval.

And she knew *he* knew.

'OK, Miss Prim,' he said. 'Let's see if you can show Paco here how to play the game.'

22

The Child of the Spirit

This time it was different. At least it seemed different to start with. No forest. No clearing. No choices. Instead she was in the room of a house. Probably the living room, judging from the furniture, though there was no sign that anybody had been living in it recently. There was an old-fashioned stove in one corner but no fire in it. There were windows but they were shuttered on the outside and a pale, cheerless light seeped through the cracks. There was an oil lamp on a table but she could see no means of lighting it, even if she knew how. All the furniture – and there was quite a lot of it – was made of bamboo and had an oriental feel. And there was a picture on the wall of a forest, with Chinese or Japanese characters on it.

As soon as she saw the forest Jade knew this was her own special starting point – but in a different guise. And sure enough, when she took a long cool look about the place there were the usual choices waiting for her – except that this time they weren't paths; they were doors. Three doors on three different walls. All closed.

She stood there for a moment in the centre of the room thinking about it. It occurred to her that she did not have to play Kobal's game. Or at least, she didn't have to make a choice. She could just stay here and see what happened next. She was fed up being pushed around and manipulated.

But he was perfectly capable of letting her stay here for ever. Or at least until she went mad with boredom.

She sighed and crossed to one of the doors. It didn't seem to matter which. There was lattice-work panelling on it with a design that showed a tree and a porcelain handle with a bird on it.

She pulled open the door . . .

And leaped back with a scream of terror.

Rearing up at her on its hind legs was a bear. Not a friendly, shambling kind of bear like Laurie but a snarling fury of a bear with vicious teeth and glaring eyes, its giant claws reaching out for her.

She retreated across the room, searching frantically for a weapon – but there was nothing. Not even an umbrella. She backed into a chair and they both went over. She lay helpless on the floor . . .

But the bear didn't move. It stayed snarling and glaring and reaching out for her. But it also stayed put.

It was stuffed.

Jade sat on the floor looking up at it with her heart trying to beat its way out of her chest.

It was in some kind of a cupboard – like a broom cupboard – and from what she could see from her position on the floor, the cupboard didn't seem to lead anywhere, even if you could have squeezed past the bear.

She climbed to her feet rubbing her bottom and pressed her head against the wall, waiting for her heart to stop pounding. Then she approached the second door. This time she wasn't so careless. She pressed her ear to the panelling and listened for a moment. Then as slowly and warily as a burglar she opened it.

It was another cupboard but it didn't seem to contain anything more threatening than a coat, a large backpack and a pair of boots.

Jade dragged out the backpack first. It was very

heavy – she could hardly have got it on her back – and when she opened the straps at the top it appeared to be full of tinned food.

And somebody had thoughtfully supplied a tin opener on the top.

Jade picked up one of the tins. *Vichyssoise*, it said. And there was a picture on the side of a bowl of green soup.

She picked up another. Also vichyssoise.

In fact, they were all vichyssoise. All thirty-six tins.

Very funny, she thought. A bear and thirty-six tins of cold, green soup. Clearly Kobal's idea of a joke.

She read the label. The main ingredients seemed to be leek and potatoes. *Serve hot or cold*, it said.

Great. Well, at least now she knew what vichyssoise was made of. Could she go home now?

She looked at the last door.

Perhaps she'd find a box of matches. Then she could light the stove. And heat up one of the tins of leek-and-potato soup.

She opened the door.

The blast of ice-cold air hit her like a blow.

She staggered back, shielding her face as a wind like a thousand demons howled into the room. The door swung violently on its hinges. And she found herself looking through her outstretched arms at the most desolate landscape she had ever seen.

It was even worse than Lake Piru.

At least Lake Piru was surrounded by forest. This had nothing. It seemed to consist solely of bare rock and patches of snow. There wasn't a single tree in sight.

Then in the distance she saw a range of snow-covered mountains. The setting sun was on them and they looked quite breathtakingly beautiful.

But a long way off.

She struggled to close the door and sat down on the floor again, a little more gently this time.

What was she supposed to do?

She couldn't go out into that. But she couldn't stay here either, eating cold leek-and-potato soup for as long as it pleased Kobal to let her.

Which was likely to be as long as the tins lasted – and some more.

Then she remembered the coat and the boots.

They were exactly her size. The coat was hooded and in the pockets were a pair of gloves and a pair of snow goggles.

Well done, Father, she thought, you think of everything.

Though it was much more likely to have been Barmella.

But whoever she had to thank for it, it was a wonderful coat. You could fasten the hood and the collar so that there was just a small slit for your eyes, and when she put the goggles on there wasn't a scrap of flesh exposed to the elements.

Thus equipped she headed once more for the door . . .

When she had caught her breath and could stand upright without hanging on to the wall she saw there was a path – of sorts – winding through the rocks and the snow in the direction of the distant mountains.

It would take days, if not weeks, to walk there. In the real world.

But cyberspace had its own rules about distance. Like in dreams.

Sometimes a very short distance would take an impossible time – like the distance up the steps to the statue of Kali when the Thugs were after her. Other times, it seemed, you could get to the moon in a leap and a bound.

Which is what it was like with the mountains.

Not exactly a leap and a bound but an hour or so of trudging along the footpath with her head and shoulders bent into the wind and the thought of all that cold green soup waiting for her if she gave up.

The path became steeper and steeper, almost like a treadmill where you can adjust the angle. She soon had to scramble on all fours. But every time she looked up the mountains were closer, and finally they loomed up all around her: great snow-covered giants with their heads in the clouds – and more clouds below, shrouding the distant valley. Bare rock on one side, a sheer drop on the other. And the track winding on, no wider than a mule at best – and at worst an average-sized goat.

At times she had to edge her way along it, step by step, with her back pressed hard against the rock, not daring to look down into the impossible void below.

But at least the wind had dropped and although the sun had long since sunk below the peaks of the mountains there was still enough light enough to see by.

Of course it had occurred to her, more than once, that she didn't have the slightest idea where she was going. There was nothing new about this. Not in the game. Not even in life, come to think of it. But usually, before very long, things started to happen. They weren't very pleasant things – in fact, mostly they were extremely unpleasant and dangerous – but at least they were happening. This time – zilch. The track just kept winding on and on with never a sign of human or even animal life. Not even a kite.

Then it began to dawn on her that she was going round in circles.

There was nothing she could put her finger on. Everything looked the same. She just had the feeling that the track was not actually going anywhere.

She stopped to think about it.

How did the game work? There was a certain element of geography built into it, depending on how much Kobal knew about the place where a particular child had been taken. The landscape, the things Jade encountered along the way – props like the stuffed bear and the tins of soup – they were all programmed. But actually getting there, actually finding the person she was supposed to be looking for – that was down to her. She *sensed* what she was looking for and where the child had been taken or hidden – and the game responded. The game became real life.

At least that's what she thought happened.

But it wasn't happening this time.

This time there seemed to be a block on her.

Instead of seeing things clearly in her head there was a kind of mist.

And as this dawned on her – a real mist began to

form. A mist in the mountains. It rose from below and wiped out the track like a large soft rubber. She was forced to edge along all the time now with her back against the cliff, making very little progress.

And she was getting tired now. Tired and hungry.

She began to feel frightened. And tearful, which was unusual.

She had this feeling that whoever it was who was blocking her had decided she was its enemy. And yet the vague sense she had of it – this *presence* – was . . . The word that sprang to mind was *good*. A good presence. A good person. Someone with whom she could be friends. Someone she could really trust; who would be on her side.

But this person didn't trust *her*.

This made her sad. Because if it was true – if this was a good person who didn't trust her . . .

She slid down the side of the rock and put her head in her hands and wept. Alone on the mountainside in the mist she wept for what she had lost and what she had become. A creature of Kobal. A weapon in whatever game he was playing.

And the child she was searching for knew it.

And didn't want to be found.

23

Mist on the River

'It's the not knowing that I can't stand.'

Emily clenched her fist against the cold stone wall of the Thames Embankment. The Gothic outline of Tower Bridge swam through a veil of mist and tears.

'Not knowing where she is or who's with her or what's happening to her. Not being able to *help* her.'

Emily raised both fists and brought them down on the wall with a force that sent a pain shooting up to her elbow. Benedict reached a sympathetic hand to her shoulder but then he saw the anger in her face and drew back.

'I'm sorry,' he said.

'You're *sorry*? But not enough to tell me where she is?'

He shrugged but his expression was sad. 'You have to trust me,' he said.

'But I *don't* trust you!'

She pressed the back of her hand to her teeth. She was too angry to choose her words with the usual care. The usual tact and diplomacy. He was her only link with Jade; she mustn't risk losing him.

But she *was* losing him. He was leaving today. Flying back to Rome, or wherever it was he came from.

It was two days since the Battle of Mistletoe Cottage. Her car was in a garage in Berkshire where puzzled mechanics shook their heads over its battered remains. The equally battered 'animals of the forest' had either vanished back into it or were being held by Benedict's 'people'. And the witch had not been seen again – at least according to him. It was entirely possible, of course, that she was in some cell of the Holy Inquisition, being tortured for her secrets.

It was *impossible* for her to trust him. She couldn't believe anything he told her. He reminded her too much of Kobal.

And yet . . . there was something in her that *wanted* to trust him. Or perhaps it was something in *him*. At least he seemed sincere, not openly mocking of himself and others, as Kobal had been.

The Kobal she had known, all those years ago, had been a games player – teasing, manipulative, forever poking sticks. Benedict wasn't like that.

But in a way she couldn't quite figure, they were so much alike.

Was it because they had both been Brothers in the same Holy Order?

This was difficult to pin down, too. In the three days since they had met she had done her homework. The Order of Saint Saviour of Antioch had been founded in 1185 – one of those mysterious brotherhoods of warrior monks like the Knights Templar. Two years later Jerusalem had fallen to the Saracens under Saladin and they'd been forced to flee with what was left of the Crusader army and they had been on the move ever since. For hundreds of years they had fought those they considered the enemies of the Church until the Church itself decided they had outlived their usefulness. But there was some mystery as to whether they had actually been disbanded. They kept turning up in odd places and in even odder roles. During the First World War they had served as ambulance drivers for the Austrians in the Carpathian Mountains, near their old haunts in Transylvania.

During the Second, they had fought for the German Resistance against Hitler and many had died in the concentration camps.

And now?

No one seemed to know. A purely ceremonial Order, some authorities said. Others hinted at a more secretive role as special agents of the Vatican. Others said they had always been independent of Rome – and often at loggerheads with the Pope of the day.

Emily was a doctor and a scientist. A geneticist. She had a deep suspicion of all religions – and religious people. Especially monks. She was prepared to accept she didn't know much about them, or their beliefs, but one thing she did know: most religions were opposed to genetic engineering – certainly of the kind that interested Kobal. His experiments would have horrified them. So what would they make of the results – Jade in particular?

Benedict would not tell her where she was. Or how he had found her. All he would say was that he had followed a trail and it had led to Kobal and that Jade was with him. Safe, for the time being.

But what if he was lying?

What if Benedict had kidnapped her? Or members of his mysterious Order? Perhaps in the hope that she would lead them to the other . . . experiments. And then what? Once they'd rounded them all up would they destroy them, as an abomination in the sight of the Lord? Or stick them away in some remote mountain convent as freaks of nature?

Emily knew she was letting her imagination – and her fears – get the better of her. But Benedict didn't help. If only he would tell her what he knew. Take her into his confidence. That was why she hammered the wall of the Embankment in her frustration.

She had grazed the side of her hand. Little spots of blood had welled up and begun to run together. She sucked them to stop them getting on her sleeve. Benedict leaned on the wall beside her with both hands, arms straight, head down between them. Anyone seeing them would think they were lovers having a quarrel.

This was one of her favourite parts of London. Directly across the river were the medieval battlements of the Tower of London – beyond that the taller towers of the City, like beacons in the mist. To the east was her own apartment on Jacob's Island – the setting for the last horrendous scene in *Oliver Twist*. She often came here to eat, in one of the restaurants along Shad Thames. Usually alone. She spent a lot of her time alone nowadays. She lived alone, ate alone . . . She had friends but she saw less and less of them. Very rarely sought them out. If she saw anyone at all it was Jade's mother. And in truth she didn't really like her very much; they had very little in common, besides their love for Jade.

And their grief.

She was so lonely. All her life, it seemed, she had been struggling to pass some kind of test. First it was the exams at school, then at university, then the much harder ones as a doctor and geneticist. Solving problems, passing tests, getting to the bottom of some mystery or another, whether it was the nature of a disease or the answer to the meaning of life. As if life itself was one great detective mystery and she had to spend large amounts of her time trying to solve it.

It had set her apart from people.

And now she had another mystery to ponder.

$$777 - \frac{777}{7} = 666$$

What did it mean?

More to the point, what did it mean for Jade?

'What if I went to the police?' she said. 'They'd arrest you. They'd certainly want to question you.'

'Yes,' he agreed.

'And you'd tell them nothing.'

'No,' he said. He raised his head and looked at her. 'For the same reason I can't tell you. Because it would put her life in danger.'

'More than it is already?'

'More than it is already.'

'You could trust me.'

He smiled sadly. 'Like you trust me?'

She flushed. 'So only you can save her?'

'I didn't say that. But I have to find out what Kobal wants with them.' He moved a little closer, dropping his voice. She felt his breath on the side of her face. 'Look, before we can move against him we have to solve the mystery of the Septagram. We have to know what his plans are, otherwise . . . we might force him into something we'd regret.'

'Oh!' She pounded the wall again with her fist, but not quite so violently.

'I'm sorry,' he said again. 'I have to follow . . . my path.'

'Your path,' she repeated bitterly.

They stood in silence for a moment as the wintry sun slid behind the south tower of the bridge. It was the first day of March – soon to be spring, but bitterly cold. The incoming tide met the current as it flowed down to the sea and whipped a murky froth off the coffee-coloured waves. It was a wind from the Northlands, splintered with ice. She shuddered.

'If it . . . if it leads me to her,' he continued hesitantly. 'If it turns out that her . . . that her heart is true, then I will send for you. Or I will send her to you.'

She turned on him sharply, her worst fears all but realized.

'What do you mean, "if her heart is true"?'

He looked at her and his eyes were more troubled than she had seen them.

'If she is not a creature of Kobal,' he said.

24

The Family

The snow was melting.

It dripped from the gutters and the gables. It dribbled from the mouths of the gargoyles that leaned out from the castle walls, first in a milky trickle and then in a steady stream. It trickled from the casements and wriggled down the windows like a torrent of silver centipedes. It slid from the steeply sloping roofs of the turrets in great white chunks and crashed down on to the rocks far below. From the window of her room, high in the west tower, Jade could see deep fissures opening in the crust of snow and ice that covered the surface of the lake. It already resembled a giant jigsaw in parts and way out in the middle, out from under the shadow of the surrounding fells, whole pieces were missing and she could see the sheen of sunlight on clear water.

Sunlight. For months on end through the long Lapland winter the sun had been banished far to the south. But now, for several hours a day it bathed the white wilderness in its life-giving radiance. A world of sparkling crystal. Not warm, not yet. Jade's breath still mistead the panes of her casement window, still steamed in the thin Arctic air when she was allowed out into the courtyard that was the limit of her icy refuge – but when she listened she could hear the sound of running water; the music of spring.

She turned away from the window and contemplated her bedroom. She was surprised she still had it to herself, with all the new arrivals they'd been getting lately.

It was three weeks since she had lost her way in the mountains. Three weeks since he came to her rescue yet again – this time by the simple means of lifting the helmet off her head and removing the electrodes from her temples. This was not advisable, he had informed her sternly. It could be dangerous. You had to play the game to the end, not sit down and cry when you lost your way.

She had not played the game since.

She needed a rest, he told her. She needed to get her strength back. But she knew this was just an excuse. When she played the game he followed her progress on computer. He knew every move she made. He knew where she was going, who she met, what she was thinking – and what conclusions she had come to. Since that last game he had hardly spoken to her. On the few occasions she had met him his manner had been distant. Cold. She knew he didn't trust her any more. She couldn't be relied upon to make the right decisions: meaning the decisions he wanted her to make. He couldn't trust her not to think for herself – and come to conclusions that were opposed to his own.

And one thing Kobal couldn't stand was opposition.

Besides, he had found someone much more reliable.

To Jade's knowledge, Paco had played the game three times – it might have been more – and each time, if recent deliveries were anything to go by, he had come back with one of Kobal's missing brood of children.

She heard the familiar scratching sound on the door.

'Come in,' she said, turning from her lonely vigil by the window as the door opened to admit the massive, shambling figure of her servant, bodyguard – and jailer.

'Hi, Laurie,' she said as the bear shambled into the room and looked at her in that strange, sidelong way he had with his sad brown eyes, as if he was ashamed of himself or the role he had to play.

'You and me both . . .' she murmured quietly to herself – but she knew what he had come for and she grabbed a towel and the bag with her gym kit and followed him out of the room and along the corridor.

Barmella was waiting for her as usual in the gym. But she was no longer alone.

The Castle of Demons was getting crowded.

'Morning, Fraulein,' Jade sang out dutifully. 'Morning, Paco. Morning, Kai. Morning, Solomon. Morning, Barega . . .'

Paco and his lost children: the missing pieces he had found on his journeys through cyberspace. His new gang.

And he ruled them just as he'd ruled the gang on the tip.

Jade still didn't know what to make of the newcomers. She hadn't had much chance to get to know them properly and she suspected this was a deliberate strategy on Kobal's part. He didn't want her putting the wrong ideas into their heads.

She liked Barega best – or perhaps it was truer to say she disliked him the least. He came from a remote part of Australia called Arnhem Land on the far north-east coast, famed as the birthplace of the didgeridoo – a wind instrument like a flute. At first Jade thought this was why Kobal called him the Child of the Wind but when she asked Barega directly he just shrugged and said it was very windy where he lived. He didn't have a lot to say for himself but there was a kind of gentleness about him that Jade liked. She guessed he had a strong streak of independence in him – but for the time being, lonely and homesick, he had attached himself to Paco.

Kai was the Child of the Sea. Paco had found her in one of the islands of the South Pacific, about a thousand miles from Hawaii. She was quite shy or withdrawn and Jade's attempts to get to know her better had been rebuffed. She couldn't help thinking that Kai would always follow whoever seemed the strongest and the most useful to her, but maybe this wasn't fair.

The one she found hardest to like was Solomon,

the Child of the Moon. He came from the Mountains of the Moon in Uganda but he had been kidnapped and forced to join a group of rebels living in the bush – and that was about all Jade knew about him. Unlike the rest of them he didn't speak much English. So he hardly spoke at all and he followed Paco like his shadow.

When Jade entered the gym they were in line abreast riding the exercise bikes while Barmella yelled a stream of instructions at them. Jade reluctantly climbed on an empty saddle. She could never understand why physical exercise was so important to Barmella – and presumably Kobal, who gave her the orders. It wasn't as if any of them were fat – though Paco was doing his best to make up for all those lean years on the tip.

They were supposed to be here to improve their minds, according to Kobal. Or rather, the special part of their minds that gave them their power.

Not that there was much sign of it in the children Paco had located on his travels in cyberspace. He'd probably just found them on the Internet, Jade thought cattily. And Kobal couldn't tell the difference.

Paco had power, though. It was hard to pin down exactly what it was but it was a kind of *controlling* power. Almost like hypnosis. More than that – the sense that if you didn't do what he wanted he'd burn you up. Your brain cells would just . . . spontaneously combust. He'd tried it with Jade. She could feel him trying to hex her. It made her feel uncomfortable but no more than that. So far she'd been able to resist him.

Of course she'd tried to use her own power on him. But he was too strong for her. She couldn't read his thoughts – and she couldn't find out what he was scared of, much less use it against him.

It disturbed her that she could even think this way. Perhaps it was part of Kobal's game plan – to pit them against each other – to see who was the strongest. If he had other plans for them, he was keeping them very quiet these days. There was no more about how they were going to save the planet.

The door opened and Shrika came in – late as usual. The Child of Magic. Shrika certainly had power, at least over animals – Jade had seen her in action in the circus ring – but she kept her talents well under wraps at Castle Piru. Like Jade she seemed to be able to resist Paco's dominance – but she hadn't made a friend of Jade, either.

So suddenly Jade had a family. And felt more alone than ever.

'Faster, faster,' shrieked Barmella, like some demented sergeant-major. Jade bent low over the handlebars and drove the pedals into a blur of speed but her thoughts were whirring almost as fast and she wasn't thinking about cycling.

She had never had any trouble making friends in the past. She had been well liked at school, so far as she could tell. She sometimes had words with the older boys who thought she was too mouthy, but that was only to be expected; they were boys. But on the whole she'd never had any problems with people her own age.

So it upset her to be cast as the castle ghost.

It made her wonder if she *was* a ghost. Not quite there. Like in the game.

Or perhaps she just had BO.

But then Paco shouldn't have any problem with that, the way he'd smelled on the tip.

Stop it, she commanded herself fiercely.

This place brought the worst out in her. She was becoming a horrible person. Maybe that was why people didn't like her; they knew what she was thinking about them.

She was beginning to lose track of herself. Sometimes, in the privacy of her own room, she would speak her name aloud, as if to remind herself who she really was. But it sounded more and more like a stranger, someone she had never really known. She was scared of losing her identity entirely. But perhaps she didn't have an identity. Perhaps she was just one of Kobal's creatures, to be moulded by him until she turned into whatever he wanted her to be.

The door was flung open and there he was.

Even by the standards he set himself it was a fairly dramatic entrance – and clearly he hadn't come for a bike ride. He wore the costume of a Cossack horseman – red tunic, fur hat, leather boots, even a horse whip – but instead of a horse he was accompanied by two of the fiercest dogs Jade had ever seen. They weren't particularly big, at least not in height, but they were bulging with muscle; their teeth stuck out over their lips and they had piggy little eyes. In fact they looked like a cross between dogs and wild boar. They were straining at the leash but Kobal didn't seem to have any trouble holding them with just one hand.

'Morning, children,' he greeted them with a smile.

'Morning, Father,' they chorused. All except Jade.

Look at him, she thought. My father.

If you could believe him.

Most of the time Jade had been growing up in Turnham Green she had never doubted her parents, never questioned them. They were just her parents. But then she had begun to view them more critically; even to wonder how she came to have them. (She thought of herself as having *them*; not of them having *her*.) She knew she was different from them. And even if she wasn't she would have tried to be. But even this gave her some sense of her own identity.

Now . . .

Now that she had found out they weren't her parents, not her real parents, and that she really was different – a kind of freak – what was she left with?

Kobal.

She looked at him posing in the doorway.

No wonder she didn't know who she was – with a father like Kobal who was a hundred different people all rolled up in one.

She had seen many sides of his personality and she couldn't say she liked any of them. He was far too weird to be liked. But in a perverse way she wanted him to like *her*. She wouldn't admit it – she could barely admit it to herself – but she wanted his approval.

And she sure as Hell wasn't getting it. Not lately.

He didn't even look at her as he strode into the room after his panting dogs.

Behind him – at a safe distance – came Laurie.

He clearly didn't like the dogs any more than he liked Kobal and he tried to hide himself in a corner. It didn't work but he kept very still. Like he was stuffed.

Kobal stood by the weight machines and for the first time Jade noticed that one of them was in a blue plastic cover, as if it had just arrived and hadn't been unwrapped yet.

'If you don't mind, Fraulein,' he said with a smile, 'I'd just like a few words while we've got everyone together.'

Barmella bowed and retired to the wall bars where, as far as Jade knew, she spent most of her leisure hours, hanging upside down like a bat.

The rest of them gathered round in a circle on the floor, well out of range of the dogs.

'Excellent,' said Kobal. 'My little *chicos*.' As usual you didn't know if he was being ironic. Enjoying a private joke.

'Some of you may have been wondering why I have brought you here,' he said.

This was true.

'I've explained something of my ambitions for you individually – but the time has come to think of yourself as a unit. A collective. The Seven. The Magnificent Seven. There is, however, one little problem. Can anyone tell me what it is?'

Only one, thought Jade. Where do I start?

It was Paco who answered.

'We're only six,' he said.

'Right,' said Kobal, as if this took real genius. 'You're only six. We are missing the seventh. And without him – we are nothing.'

So that was it.

They had to be seven to add up to anything. At least in Kobal's eyes.

But why?

'You have all tried to find the seventh,' he said.

This was news to Jade. They'd *all* tried. And yet none of them ever talked about it, at least not to her.

'And you've all failed.'

So why did he seem to blame Jade in particular?

'The time has come,' he said, 'to try a new approach. To adopt new methods, new strategies. We are engaged in a noble endeavour, *mes enfants*. We are fighting a war – and it is a war we must win.'

He sounded like a politician. In fact he sounded

like one politician in particular: Winston Churchill. Another act. Jade wasn't sure it worked while he was dressed as a Cossack. One of the dogs whined and Kobal kicked it.

'You are all under sentence of death,' he informed them.

For a moment Jade thought he meant from him. But no, he meant from the Enemy.

He had told them about the *Sami* in the forest. Blinded by ancient superstition, they were resolved to burn Castle Piru to the ground. And everyone in it. Worse, they had joined forces with a gang of fanatical monks who were pledged to destroy them as the spawn of Satan.

'With the melting of the snows,' he continued, 'an attack is imminent. We must fight terror with terror.'

What did he mean? Or was it just words?

'With an enemy so deadly, so determined – we must act with utter ruthlessness.'

He stepped to one side and unveiled the machine behind him.

It was not a weight machine at all.

It was a cage.

But there was nothing in it.

He opened the door.

'Lours,' he said, crooking a finger. 'Come here.'

Oh no, thought Jade. She put her fist to her mouth.

The bear shambled out of its corner. The dogs snarled and showed their teeth.

'In,' said Kobal.

With something that sounded very much like a groan, Laurie stepped into the cage.

Kobal shut the door and locked it.

'Now,' he said. 'Fraulein Sophie – if you please.'

Barmella came down from the wall bars and picked up a box that was lying on the floor. She carried it over and gave each of them something that looked like a television remote.

'Paco. You will be the first. Step up here if you please.'

Paco stepped up to where Kobal was standing a little to the side of the cage.

'Now – point the remote at the cage and press the red button.'

Paco didn't hesitate.

The bear gave a little leap into the air. Paco laughed harshly. Jade bit into her knuckle until she drew blood.

'The floor of the cage is electrified,' explained

Kobal. 'Every time you press the button it delivers a mild electric shock through the soles of the bear's feet. You can increase the force of the shock and how long it lasts by pressing these buttons here. Once more if you please, Senor Paco.'

It was horrible. Laurie leaped from one foot to the other as Paco pressed the buttons.

Jade stood up. At least she started to stand up but she found Barmella's hand on her shoulder. 'Sit,' hissed Barmella.

'Behold,' said Kobal, 'the dancing bear.'

He made each of them do it in turn. After Paco came Kai, then Solomon, then Barega . . .

Barega didn't seem too keen. He stared at the bear – then at Kobal – then at the remote.

'Press the button, Barega,' said Kobal.

But he wouldn't. He just kept staring at the remote.

'He can't feel anything,' Kobal assured him. 'He's a robot. I made him myself.'

'If he can't feel anything why is he dancing?' shouted Jade from the floor. She was in tears.

'He *likes* dancing, don't you, boy?' said Kobal. Then he looked at Jade. 'It's a sensory reaction. But he feels no pain. He's like a headless chicken. So, off you go,

Barega – make him dance.'

So Barega made him dance.

'Now Shrika,' said Kobal.

Shrika got up, walked up to where Kobal was standing, pressed the button once, then walked back and sat down. There was something insolent in the whole operation.

Kobal looked as if he was going to call her back but then thought better of it.

'Now Jade,' he said. 'Your turn.'

But Jade just shook her head.

'I told you Jade – he feels no pain. Come and make him dance.'

But Jade didn't believe him.

And even if he was telling the truth she didn't want to make Laurie dance. It was undignified.

Kobal walked towards her with the dogs. He stopped and looked down at her. The dogs were right in her face. She could smell their foul breath. She turned her head away. Barmella's hand was still on her shoulder.

'This is what the Enemy did for amusement,' said Kobal. His voice was soft but there was something deadly about it. 'Throughout history they amused themselves by tormenting and torturing animals.

They still do.' He glanced towards the solitary window high in the wall. 'And by the Enemy I don't just mean the men in the forest out there. I mean the human race.'

Jade looked up at him. Wasn't *he* a member of the human race? Weren't they all?

'This is what we are up against,' he continued. 'This is what we are fighting. And if we are to win we have to be as ruthless – as unfeeling – as they are. Jade, make the bear dance.'

Jade looked him right in the face and shook her head.

It was impossible to read the expression in his eyes.

'So. You defy me.' His voice was still soft but there was no hiding the menace in it. 'Very well. I won't punish you. Not directly. But we all have to know the consequences of our actions. If not to ourselves, then to others.

'I will show you what else they did to bears.'

25

The Bear Pit

The temperature had dropped during the night and it had begun to snow. Not the violent snows of winter but large, wet flakes drifting gently down from the heavens as if to bind the wounds caused by the recent thaw. Pleasant enough to watch through a hole in the misted window with a log fire crackling in the open hearth and a warm bed waiting.

But not for Jade.

She gazed down at the huddled figure in the courtyard below and watched the snow settling on his matted fur. The bear had been chained to a stake directly opposite Jade's bedroom window so she could see him whenever she chose to look – and reflect on the price of rebellion. In the morning, at sun up, she would join the others in the courtyard and watch the dogs tear him to pieces.

Bear-baiting, Kobal called it. A 'sport' in which six dogs were pitted against a single bear – after it was first chained to a stake and muzzled.

'In the old days they would have pulled out its claws too,' Kobal had told them, 'but I don't think we need go to such extremes.'

No. They got the point.

This was a history lesson. To teach them what human beings were like when they were allowed to indulge their basic instincts. This was what they did for entertainment in the days before television and cinema and football matches.

'And would do again,' Kobal assured them, 'given half the chance.'

So this was part of their education.

'First, know thine enemy,' he told them, 'then plan how you're going to beat the pants off of him.'

But to do that they needed discipline. They needed sacrifice. And most of all they needed unity.

Jade pressed her forehead against the cold glass of the window and closed her eyes, shutting out the sight of the forlorn figure in the snow.

This was more than a history lesson. This was

about Kobal and her. Father and daughter. This was to teach *her* a lesson.

But why? What did he have against her? It was more than refusing to make a bear dance. Was it because of her failure to find the Seventh Child – did he think it was deliberate?

'You are the only one who can do this for us,' he had told her. 'You are the eldest – and the strongest.'

Or was it because of the mysterious monk who had helped her fight the Thugs in the Temple of Kali? As if she had conjured him up with her own will.

So he would bend her will to his. And make her his creature. Like Paco.

She opened her eyes and focused on the solitary figure in the silent courtyard. Another of Kobal's creatures. A robot. *Who could feel no pain.* And who would be destroyed because he was her friend. Her only friend in the Castle of Demons.

'No!' She spat the word aloud against the misted glass of the window. Not if she could help it.

She turned away from the window.

She had to put a stop to this.

But how?

The whole castle was filled with security cameras. Cameras and spies. Even in her own bedroom.

She confronted the massed array of mobiles hanging down from the ceiling. Model aircraft and helicopters and butterflies and birds and bats and even little dragons with wings. All of them seemed to be watching her – and she had no doubt that at least some of them were.

They were supposed to be toys. Cunningly designed by Kobal for her amusement. All she had to do was flick them with her finger and they would go soaring around the room – until she stopped them with a whistle. Or their batteries ran down.

Or their batteries ran down.

Of course. She ran round the room jumping up at them and flicking them one by one with her finger until the whole room was alive with flying, soaring, skimming, diving plastic toys. Then she lay down on her bed and waited. Five minutes. Ten. She felt dizzy watching them. Then, one by one, they began to drop. It took another five minutes before the last of them hit the deck.

Jade sat up. The floor was littered with plastic bodies.

'That will teach you to spy on me,' Jade instructed them calmly.

She picked her way carefully through the corpses

and opened the door to her dressing room. Inside were hundreds of costumes on rails. These, too, had been provided by Kobal for her amusement, doubtless because he thought people were all as mad as he was for dressing up. She'd never even tried them on. It wasn't her thing. Not for years. But she knew what was here because she'd looked through them when she first came here, marvelling at his extravagance. And there was something that would be very useful to her now.

A few minutes later a small hooded figure in a black robe emerged from Jade's room and padded slowly down the corridor. No one would have mistaken it for Kobal – but they wouldn't have thought it was Jade either. They'd never seen her dressed as a monk before. It might have been one of the creatures he kept in his dungeons and let out at night to prowl around the corridors so everyone else stayed safely in their rooms.

She reached the narrow arch that led to the stairs – the stone spiral stairs that connected every floor in the castle. Her bedroom was on the third floor. On the ground floor there was a door leading into the courtyard. It was kept locked at night but the key hung on a hook on the wall at the side, in case of fire.

She took it down and turned the lock.

Then she paused.

Was this just a little too easy?

Another test perhaps, to see how far she would go in defying him.

Too bad. She pulled open the door and stepped out into the little courtyard.

It was formed by three of the castle walls and an outer wall above the lake – like a well or a pit. A bear pit.

The bear lifted its muzzle and let out a soft growl. Jade crossed the courtyard towards it. The bear scrambled to its feet and showed its teeth.

It was not a welcoming grin. It was a snarl.

Jade threw back her hood. 'It's all right, Laurie,' she hissed. 'It's me. Jade.'

She was close enough to touch him. And he could have cracked her skull with a single blow. The snow had melted almost as soon as it landed on him and his fur was soaking wet. He watched her dully. It was impossible to tell if he trusted her – or just didn't care.

The chain was almost too heavy for her to pick up. One end was wrapped round the bear's neck, the other around the stake and secured by a massive padlock. And this time there was no key hanging from a hook.

She pulled at it feebly. But if Laurie couldn't break it, what chance did she have? She'd have to find the key.

Where could it be? Kobal's study?

Hopeless if it was. The door was always locked, even when he was in the room. It was a combination lock and he was probably the only one who knew the code; certainly Jade didn't.

His bedroom? But she had no idea where he slept, even after four months here.

But thinking about it coolly – and she *was* cool out in that courtyard – it seemed unlikely that Kobal would have locked up the bear personally. He didn't do things like that. He let the servants do it.

The strange thing was – you didn't often see the servants. You just sensed they were around. Or you saw the results of their work – like the fire in her bedroom or the candles and the torches that were constantly replaced.

The only servant Jade saw regularly was Laurie, who seemed to have been given the special responsibility of looking after the children, when he wasn't scheduled to be torn apart by dogs.

But it seemed likely that other servants had chained him to the stake – powerful servants at that, just in case he decided to object.

Kobal might have supervised the operation – but would he have kept the key?

It was useless. She was going around in circles.

How could you find a key in a castle? A castle full of locked doors.

Think, she commanded herself sternly.

Perhaps she could pick the lock.

She examined it carefully. The keyhole was so big she could put her little finger in it. She poked around experimentally. People were always picking locks on television and in films. Even the most unlikely people seemed to be good at it.

But not Jade. She didn't have the faintest idea how to pick a lock. She might just as well try to pick someone's pocket.

Or their brains.

It came to her in a flash as she stood there in the snow.

She could pick people's brains.

But whose? Who would know where the keys were kept?

Barmella.

Of course. Barmella was the general housekeeper – as well as nurse, gym instructor and resident bat-person.

But she'd tried reading Barmella's thoughts once before and it hadn't worked. Worse, Barmella had known what she was doing and it had landed Jade in serious trouble. In fact, it had landed her where she was now.

Still – what else could she do?

She leaned against the stake and put her hand to her head and tried to concentrate while the bear watched her dully and the breath rose from his wet muzzle.

Pictures began to form in her mind. Barmella in her leotard and tights hanging from the wall bars in the gym. Barmella lifting weights. Barmella on the exercise bike at 30 mph and maximum incline. Was she really in the gym at this time of night – just on midnight – or was this just Jade's memory of her?

Concentrate. Fiercely she projected herself into Barmella's thoughts . . .

Then she began to hear things. Snatches of sound or signals as if she was scanning the wavelengths on a radio. Meaningless garbage . . .

Then . . .

'*Dreizehn, veirzehn, funfzehn . . .*'

It sounded like someone counting. It if was Barmella she was probably doing sit-ups, or chin-ups or press-ups. At a quarter to midnight.

It figured.

'The key,' Jade prompted her. 'Where did you put the key?'

She had a terrible feeling of déjà vu. And she knew why. The last time she had tried something like this it had been with Barmella's car keys. And that had been a disaster.

'*Der schlussel?*'

The voice broke in on her own thoughts. But what did it mean?

'The key,' Jade insisted. 'Where did I put the key?'

Oh no. That was wrong. Too obvious. Besides, surely she'd be thinking in German. Don't you always think in your own language?

But then suddenly she was getting something. It was as if Barmella had started to worry about it, right out of the blue: where did she put the key? – And then she remembered. In Jade's own mind it was like a picture of a tunnel. No, not a tunnel. A corridor. A passage – with doors on each side. Doors with small barred windows, like cells. And at the end of the passage – keys. Row upon row of keys hanging from metal hooks on the wall . . .

Then there was a flash and the picture went blank. Like a TV or computer screen when it's switched off or you lose the power. And Jade knew that Barmella was on to her.

But had she realized what Jade was up to?

A savage pain ripped through her skull. So sharp and sudden she cried out in pain and clutched her head with both hands.

She stood there in the snow holding on to each side of her skull as if it was going to split down the middle. The bear growled softly and she felt his wet fur brushing against the back of her hands. Then, gradually, the pain began to ease. It was still there, grumbling away at the back of her head, but she could think clearly again and she knew she had to get to the keys before Barmella realized what was going on.

But where were they?

A long passage with doors on each side like cells . . .

The dungeons.

It had to be. She'd never been there but she knew

there was another floor below the garage with the killer cars. Kobal had told her never to go down there. He said they were the old castle dungeons where he had his laboratory – where he did his experiments and kept his animals, like the dogs she'd seen him with this morning . . .

And other things she didn't care to think about.

But how could she find it?

There was the lift in the sunroom that had taken her to the garage. But even if she could get into the sunroom, past the Flamingos Who Never Slept, she'd never find the hidden switches for the lift, not in the dark – and she daren't put the lights on.

But there must be a staircase. There was one going up. There had to be one going down.

She reached up to the bear's face and fumbled with the straps that held the muzzle in place. At least she could give him his teeth, if he wanted to fight.

'Hang on in there,' she instructed him, as if he had any choice in the matter. 'I'll be right back.'

Then she was gone – across the courtyard and back into the castle.

And there was the staircase, spiralling down into the darkness.

Nothing to stop her going down there — except her own fear.

She took a deep breath and descended. Step by step, feeling the way with her hands on the walls. Into the pit.

She reached the next floor down. The Museum of the Killer Cars. She couldn't see them but she could smell them. And sense them in the darkness. A brooding sense of menace — and death. She kept on going down the next flight. Clinging to the walls and reaching cautiously down with her feet, expecting any moment to find there was no step. Only the abyss. Then there was a light. A torch in a sconce on the wall — and a door. A wooden door with a heavy iron ring. She took hold of it with both hands, twisted and pulled. Nothing. Twisted the other way and pushed. It opened with a loud creak. She froze. Pushed again, inch by inch. Just enough to slip through the tiny gap — and she was facing a long passage with doors on each side, just like the picture in her brain. And there at the far end was a wooden board with row upon row of keys.

It was like something in the game. Should she enter the passage and search among the keys? Or was it a trap?

No choice. This time it wasn't a game.

She crept silently down the corridor. There was a strong earthy, animal smell. Like in a zoo. Each of the doors had a small barred window, set very high so she could only look in on tiptoes. But she didn't want to look in. Whatever animals were in there, she didn't want to see them. And she certainly didn't want to wake them.

Let sleeping dogs lie.

The phrase came out of nowhere. One of her foster mother's. She was always using phrases like that, wise little sayings or maxims. *Curiosity killed the cat. I want doesn't get. Pity the poor child who always gets what she wants.*

Not now. Concentrate.

And don't look through the bars.

She reached the end of the passage. It turned sharply to the right and there was a door at the end with a light coming from under it. She could hear a hum of electricity – or some sort of machinery. What was it?

But she didn't want to know. All she wanted was the key to Laurie's lock.

There were five rows of hooks with five hooks in each row. And on each hook a key – or a bunch of keys on a ring. There must have been a hundred of them. But she was looking for a big key. One big key. A key the width of her little finger.

She checked the single keys first. Only ten of them, all carefully labelled, some with names on, some with numbers. They meant nothing to her. But there were only three keys that could possibly fit the lock on Laurie's chain. She took them all and retreated back along the corridor. She had almost reached the door when . . .

Her curiosity got the better of her.

What kind of animals did Kobal keep in these rooms? Not dogs, surely. They'd be in kennels. It must be something much bigger . . .

Then she heard a sound. A very human sound. Like someone snoring. Or murmuring softly in sleep.

What if they weren't animals at all?

What if they were prisoners?

Curiosity killed the cat.

But it was no good. She'd never been very good at taking any notice of her foster mother.

She stood on tiptoe and peered through the bars of the nearest door.

She was looking into a small room – a cell – about three or four metres square, dimly lit by the flickering light of the torch at the end of the corridor. She could just make out a bed at the far end – perhaps not a bed: more a kind of shelf or platform. And there was a figure lying on it. Animal or human.

It *looked* human.

Then suddenly it awoke.

It swung its legs down to the floor and sat on the bed staring at her.

It *was* human. A man. She could just make out the shape of his head if not his features.

For a moment they just stared at each other. She could see the whites of his eyes in the shadow that was his face.

'Are you a prisoner?' she whispered.

Daft question.

He stood up and said something to her, but in a strange, guttural tongue she couldn't understand.

She couldn't leave him here. She had to let him out. But that meant finding another key . . .

He came towards her, shuffling, half stooped . . . The light spilled on to his face. He was a young man, a boy even, only a few years older than she was, but there was something in his expression, something in his eyes that warned her. They were the eyes of a zombie. She let go of the bars and hurled herself backwards just as he reached out for her. He screamed like a monkey. A scream of pure animal rage. And Jade stared up in horror at the pale hands reaching out at her through the bars and the long nails, like claws, at the end of them.

Pandemonium from the other cells. Screeches and howls and deeper, grunting growling noises . . .

Jade turned and fled. Through the door, up the stairs − as if all the demons of Hell were at her heels − up through the Museum of Killer Cars, up the next flight of stairs and out into the courtyard . . .

Laurie growled a greeting − but she thought he looked anxious. She tried the first key. No. The second. It fitted the lock but it wouldn't turn. She tried both ways but it was no good. The third . . .

A light went on. She looked up. A light in one of the windows high on the castle walls. And then another. She tried the third key. Again it fitted the lock but it wouldn't turn.

She was in despair but she forced herself to try again. The second key. This time she eased it back a little in the lock. Nothing. Then . . . a click.

The padlock sprang open.

In a fever of fear and impatience now she threaded the catch through the link in the chain . . .

And the bear was free.

The chain hung down from his neck, trailing in the snow at his feet.

But what now?

She looked up. The tall bulk of the caste rose above her on three sides. On the fourth was the wall bordering the lake. At least ten metres high and topped with razor wire. But there was a door – a portal. She remembered seeing it once on her excursions here with Laurie. A small door set in the stone at ground level – under ground level in fact because you had to go down three or four steps to reach it. She'd even asked Barmella about it and she'd told her it was a postern gate; used by the castle garrison in previous times to make a foray against the enemy or to fetch water from the lake when they were besieged.

Locked, of course. Two heavy bolts, both padlocked.

Perhaps one of the other keys . . . But she knew at first glance they wouldn't work. The locks were half the size of the one that had secured Laurie. The keys must be back in the castle . . . She groaned aloud in her despair. Then she felt a large wet paw on her shoulder. She looked up and there was Laurie, still with the chain hanging down from his neck. He pushed her gently to one side, bent his muzzle close to the lock – then he stood back and whacked it with his paw. The door shook but the lock held. Again – and again. But he couldn't get a decent hit on the lock and his paw was bleeding. Jade tugged at the fur on his arm and pointed urgently. He might not be able to break the lock but the metal barrel that secured the bolt was a different matter. It was a hefty enough affair but it was only screwed into the wood of the doorframe. And the wood was very old. Laurie hit it with one smashing blow and it splintered clear of the wood. Then he took out the second bolt.

Jade wrenched the door open and stepped outside. Outside the castle walls for the first time in four long months.

She was among trees. Small firs, two or three metres high, planted in a clump – probably to hide the postern gate – beyond them she could see rocks covered in a thin layer of snow . . . and then the lake.

It seemed to be covered in ice again – but as they scrambled over the rocks towards it she saw that there were large areas of slush. The ice that was left might take her weight – but it would never take the bear's.

The only other way was across the bridge.

She surveyed it warily. It was the only link between castle and shore. There had to be security cameras — even guards. No. It would have to be the ice.

Perhaps Laurie could swim.

Then she saw the boat. A punt or skiff. Flat-bottomed, moored at the foot of the bridge. Probably used for fishing in the summer.

Laurie looked doubtful. But after a bit of snuffling and grunting he scrambled in. The boat rocked wildly but it didn't capsize and it didn't sink. Jade untied the rope and clambered in after him. The water was almost over the sides but they were afloat. No poles, of course, or oars — that was too much to expect. She began to paddle with her hands in the icy water. Even with her gloves on it was shockingly cold. After a few seconds she felt as if her fingers would break off like icicles — and the boat had hardly moved.

But Laurie caught on fast. He squatted in the middle of the boat and used his arms like two large paddles. They made a lot of noise and they didn't exactly skim through the water but they moved, smashing through the patches of thin ice with Jade guiding him by touching one arm and then the other to steer a course roughly parallel to the bridge until finally they grounded on the shore.

It wasn't dry land exactly – but it was land.

For the first time in four months she was outside Castle Piru. A fugitive. Dressed like a monk with a bear for her only companion. And not the slightest idea where to go next.

But she was out.

And as far as she could tell, unless Kobal was playing the cruellest of practical jokes, no one had noticed.

26

Pursuit

They kept to the edge of the lake because it was the only track they could see in the dark. The bear shambled ahead on all fours, his nose close to the ground, with Jade straggling behind stumbling over the roots and rocks hidden under the fresh layer of snow.

She wondered what Kobal would do when he discovered she was gone. He'd try to get her back – of that she was certain. He'd made it painfully clear that he wanted all his children together: all seven of them. The only question was what action he'd take. Would he send the dogs after her – or come himself and attempt gentle persuasion?

'I don't think so,' she muttered to herself as she stumbled after the bear.

Her only chance was to hide in the forest. But the trees were packed close and it was no use blundering around in the dark hoping to find a footpath. She wanted to put as much distance as possible between her and the castle before daybreak.

After an hour or so the snow began to ease off and then stopped altogether, leaving the trees dusted with a thin powder as if someone had sprayed them for Christmas.

Jade wasn't too cold except for her hands. She wore several layers of clothing under her monk's robe but her gloves were soaking wet from being dipped in the lake and her fingers felt numb to the bone. She was desperately tired. She knew she was holding the bear back but whenever he pushed too far ahead he would stop and wait for her, his head tilted at an inquiring angle.

'Go on,' she shouted to him once, waving her hand at him as if to say *shooo*. But he just watched her patiently and waited until she'd caught up and then set off again at that steady, shambling pace.

The sky grew lighter. When she looked back she could see the dark shape of the castle across the lake with a single light high in the east tower. She wondered if it was Kobal's room and if he was awake, perhaps even watching her through his night glasses . . . Or reading her thoughts, amused by her little adventure. Letting her get so far before he sent the dogs after her – and whatever else he chose from his evil bestiary. She knew they had to leave the lake – but the forest presented an impenetrable barrier and despite the recent thaw the snow lay in deep folds under the canopy of firs.

The bear had stopped again. But not for her. He had found something. It looked as if it had once been a shelter or a hide, some man-made thing of branches and a dark material that might have been reindeer skin, but it had collapsed in on itself and was part covered in snow. She saw a bottle and a broken plate in among the debris but no other sign of life. The bear snuffled around for a bit and then stood on his hind legs and growled deep in his throat but Jade could see no obvious reason for anger or alarm. They carried on . . . And within a hundred metres or so they found what Jade had been looking for ever since they had left the castle – a clear track running back into the forest like a ski trail. At last they would be able to get away from the lake.

They pressed on between the tall silent firs but the track was still deep in snow and Jade found it heavy going. Every few steps she would sink up to her knees and soon she was breathing heavily and sweating under the layers of clothing. She would have given anything for a pair of snowshoes or skis. The bear was constantly stopping for her now and she urged him again to make his own escape but he just looked at her patiently and waited for her to catch up and then plodded on. And yet he'd changed from the docile creature of Castle Piru. She couldn't explain how but he seemed less of a servant; more of a bear. A wild animal of the forest. It was something in his manner, in his eyes, perhaps. And of course this was the first time she had seen him on all fours. In the castle he always walked on his hind legs.

He was limping though and there was a trail of blood in the snow. His front paw was bleeding from his fight with the door. Once, when she caught up with him, she reached out to look at it but he growled and pulled it away. It was a moment before she realized the significance of this. Despite what Kobal had told them he clearly felt pain. She worried that the blood would make it easier to follow them but it probably made little difference. Looking back she could see a clear trail of footprints through the snow.

On they went with the darkness visibly retreating before them as if it was creeping back into the forest. The track became much steeper and she was forced to scramble on all fours like the bear. They must be climbing one of the fells that surrounded the lake but she had no idea what was on the far side. She had seen no maps of the area. Whenever she had tried to find one on the computer she had found herself blocked by a window asking for her password. All Kobal had told her was that they were in a remote area of Lapland, not far from the Russian border – a land of reindeer herders, people of primitive superstitions who believed the castle to be haunted and its occupants either demons or possessed by them.

'They think I'm Count Dracula,' Kobal had told her dryly, 'and you're Dracula's daughter. They'd kill us if they could. They'd drive a stake through my heart and burn you for a witch.'

And who could blame them? She could imagine their reaction if she walked into one of their villages dressed in a monk's robe with a bear at her side. But this was the least of her worries. For the moment it was enough to keep moving, to get as far from the castle as possible.

They had reached a sloping ridge that seemed to lead to the top of the fell. She could see the summit ahead of her: a jumble of rocks rising from the trees and shaped a bit like a bird – an eagle, perhaps. The ground sloped sharply away to their right and although they were still climbing the going was not so tough. The trees had thinned out a little and looking back she could see the lake far below. But not the castle. Then she heard a sound that chilled the sweat on her body.

The howl of a wolf. Not so distant. She stopped and listened, her heart thudding in her ribs. Then more. Answering howls from further off, back along the lake towards the castle. The bear rose on his hind legs, showing his teeth. Jade scrambled up the ridge towards him. Ahead she could see the bare rock rising above the trees. It was like three rocks fused together – a rounded head flanked by two wings. But she didn't think of an eagle now: she thought of an angel. An angel with head bent in prayer, brooding down over the lake of demons. She felt that if she could only reach it she would be safe. Deep down she knew this was a hope born of despair but she struggled on regardless.

They came to another gap in the trees and looking

down she saw something moving at the edge of the lake. It looked like a bear – a brown bear of the forest – but there was something different about the way it moved. It was on all fours like Laurie but its gait was more of a scuttle . . . darting forward and then stopping to raise its long muzzle, as if sniffing the wind. What did it remind her of? Then it came to her. A chimpanzee. Or . . . a baboon.

But how could that be? *In Lapland*?

Unless it was one of Kobal's creations – a freak, like she was.

Then she heard the wolves again, closer now, much closer.

Terror revived her flagging strength. She plunged on, almost running now, falling and picking herself up, sobbing in fear and frustration. Laurie had stopped again to wait for her. He stood on his hind legs, looking back down the trail.

'Run,' she screamed at him. 'Go, go . . . Save yourself.'

But he didn't seem to understand. When she reached him he dropped on all fours but instead of moving off as he usually did he just stood there looking at her.

'Come *on*.' She tugged at the fur on his shoulder. 'Move.'

But he was like a rock.

'What is it?' She demanded. 'What's the matter with you? Do you want to die?'

She collapsed in the snow beside him. If he wasn't going to move nor would she. He growled and rolled his head and his shoulders from one side to the other as if he had a stiff neck.

Then she realized. He wanted her to climb on his back.

She clambered on, clutching at the chain round his neck with both hands. And then he began to run.

She was a city girl. She had hardly ever ridden a horse. And now she was riding a bear – bareback.

It wasn't easy. A bear, her survival book had informed her, could run as fast as a horse. Which was why it was no good trying to run away from one.

But there had been no tips on how to ride the thing.

Laurie ran with a lurching, swaying motion, the muscles rippling under his fur. It was a bit like riding a flying carpet, but at least there was something to hold on to. She lay almost full length along his back, digging her knees and her feet into his flanks and clinging desperately to the chain around his neck. The Angel Rock rose above them, very close now. But there was no sanctuary there. She couldn't think now why it had seemed so important to her.

Just before the rock the ground levelled out and even dipped a little. The bear altered his gait. He seemed to be bounding now, almost rolling like a large furry ball over the snow. Then suddenly she was flying through the air.

She landed in a deep pile of snow and struggled up, shaken but unhurt. Laurie had stopped, rising up on his hind legs. She managed to grin at him to show there were no bones broken but he was looking past her, back down the trial, with his lips drawn back from his teeth – and it wasn't a grin.

She looked back down the trail and her heart seemed to leap into her throat. Bounding towards them, no more than two or three hundred metres away, was a wolf.

It was big. Bigger than it had any right to be in this part of the world. And it was fast. It came up that slope like a greyhound on the final stretch.

Wolves, Jade had read in her survival guide, rarely if ever attack humans.

But this wolf clearly hadn't read the same book.

It ignored the bear and came straight for her. She

scrambled to her feet and raised her hands as it leaped . . .

The bear's paw caught it in mid-air and sent it hurtling into the snow.

It lay there for a moment, its long black tongue lolling from its teeth, its flanks heaving. Then its eyes glazed and it lay still.

Jade sank to her knees and looked up at Laurie in astonishment. She could see now why Kobal had ordered him chained and muzzled before the dogs were set on him.

But the wolf was not alone. There were more of them bounding up the trail – five or six at least – and behind them something even more terrifying.

It was the creature she had seen by the lake. Like a cross between a baboon and a hyena but far bigger than either. The size of a gorilla or a large bear. And its face was white. White, with a mane of thick, black hair extending halfway down its back. But the thing that really caught Jade's eye were its teeth . . .

The wolves had stopped in a half circle and the creature came running through them. It ran like one of the great apes, bounding forward on its long arms right up to where Jade knelt in the snow with the bear standing protectively over her. Then it rose on its hind legs, opened its great jaws to show the full armoury of its teeth – with two great fangs or incisors the size of daggers – and screeched like a banshee.

The wolves rushed in.

Jade turned and ran blindly towards Angel Rock. But she'd hardly taken a few steps when she felt a violent blow in her back, hurling her into the snow. She rolled over at once but the wolf was on her, a snarling fury of fur and fangs. She tried to fight but it had its front paws on her chest, its weight bearing her down, its teeth right in her face. The saliva dripped from its lolling tongue and she could smell the foul stench of its breath. Some instinct told her to stop fighting, to lie still. And it just stood there, pinning her down, staring into her face. And she knew it was one of Kobal's creatures, sent to find her, not to kill.

It was the bear they had come to kill.

She put her head to one side to escape the sight and the smell of the brute and she saw Laurie trapped in a circle of wolves. One of them leaped but he struck with that massive paw and the wolf went flying through the air. The rest drew back, crouching on their bellies or circling for an opening.

Then the creature came forward . . .

It was strangely bandy-legged, tapering to the hindquarters like a gorilla, but even so it was at least a metre taller than the bear and much wider at chest and shoulders. It opened its great jaws again and screeched – or was it a laugh? – and Laurie went for it in a shambling run, swiping with both paws at the baboon face. One of the wolves darted in and snapped at his heels and he almost stumbled and fell.

Jade knew there could be only one end to such a contest. She had freed the bear from the stake only to see him torn apart on a hill in the forest – and then they would take her back to the Castle of Demons . . . and Kobal.

27

The Shaman

Benedict had been travelling non-stop for twenty-four hours. But not to Rome, as Emily had been led to expect. Instead he took the early-morning flight from Heathrow to Helsinki where he transferred to a Finnish internal flight for the trip north. He arrived at Kittila – in Lapland – just as it was getting dark.

Jussa Proksi was waiting for him at the airport. A tall, gaunt man who could have been anything between forty and sixty, with startlingly blue eyes and a weathered complexion, pitted as if by chips of ice. He was a leader of the *Sami*, one of the oldest native peoples in Europe whose forefathers had been hunters and herders in Scandinavia for thousands of years and were now scattered over the far north of

Norway and Sweden, Finland and the Kola Peninsula in Russia – the lands of ice and snow, of forest and frozen lake.

Jussa was a member of the local Sami Parliament – the *Samitigge* – and a respected historian, but Benedict knew him to be a shaman, a wise man, steeped in the ancient religion of the *Sami* with its beliefs in the gods and demons of the forest, the powers of light and of darkness. For all their differences, the *Sami* shaman and the monk from Rome had much in common.

They drove north through the night, catching up on each other's news. It was mostly bad. The monk told the shaman of his failure with the Witch of Windsor, as he called her, and the shaman told the monk of his failure to keep a close watch on the Castle of Demons – after losing two of his watchers in a murderous attack.

'The men are very angry,' he told Benedict gravely. 'They are ready for war.'

'Time enough for that,' said Benedict, 'when we find out what's going on there.'

They reached the shaman's village in the early hours of the morning and set off at once for the lake by snowmobile, its headlights carving a ghostly path through the forest in the drifting snow. As they neared the lake they abandoned the noisy vehicle for trail skis and the shaman took them on a short-cut over one of the fells that would bring them close to the scene of the slaughter.

'Not that there's anything to see,' he grumbled before they set off. 'We took away what was left of them – which was little enough.'

'I want to see the castle,' Benedict insisted, 'from where they were hidden.'

The shaman shrugged as if to say much good it would do him.

'I have to try and make contact with the children,' Benedict told him, feeling he owed the man some explanation given the risk he was taking. 'Or one of them at least.'

Jussa Proksi said nothing but he knew that Benedict meant something more than sending them a text message. They both had their secret skills and they had learned not to ask too many questions – aloud at least.

They skied through the forest for almost an hour before Benedict saw the fell rising above them through the trees. It was crowned by a distinctive rock that glowed almost amber in the light of the rising sun. He thought it looked like an angel, kneeling in prayer.

28

The Battle of Angel Rock

They came without warning from behind the rock. The first Jade saw of them was when they came flying over the ridge – so fast that for a moment they *were* flying – and landed right in the middle of the wolf pack.

One of the men fell awkwardly and lay on his side, trying to free his boots from their bindings, but the other came to a sliding halt in a great spray of snow and was out of his skis in a flash, reaching for the rifle on his shoulders.

But the ape creature was faster. As the wolves scattered to left and right it went straight for the man with the gun. The first blow sent the rifle soaring; the second caught the man high in the head and pitched him senseless in the snow. Then a shot rang out. Jade saw the beast stagger slightly and then spin round, glaring furiously. The other man had fired from the ground with the rifle held awkwardly across his body. He brought it up to his shoulder to fire again but Jade saw the wolf out of the corner of her eye and shouted a warning. Too late. The wolf leaped and sank its teeth into the man's arm, spoiling his shot and rolling with him in the bloodied snow. Jade saw the flash of a knife – but the ape was already bounding towards them, splitting the air with its infernal screech.

She was still pinned down by her own wolf but, freed from his attackers, Laurie came charging to her rescue. He scooped the heavy animal off her as if he was catching salmon in a stream and hit it again when it came springing back, breaking its neck with a single blow. But two others were snapping at his heels and the others not far behind. Jade was already scrambling for the rifle lying in the snow. She had never handled a gun before, much less fired one but she knew how to point it and pull the trigger. What she didn't know was that the rifle was an automatic and that if she kept her finger on the trigger it would keep firing until the magazine was empty.

The gun veered off to the right as she fired and

only two of the eight shots hit the ape creature as it bounded towards the man on the ground. They didn't kill it but two eight millimetre bullets in the backside were something of a distraction. Enough for the man to knife the wolf in the neck, pick up his own gun and fire three more bullets into the creature towering above him. It reared up for a moment to its full height, clawed at its chest and then fell backwards into the snow.

The surviving wolves turned and fled.

Jade dropped the empty gun and fell to her knees. She felt drained suddenly as if the last surge of adrenalin had exhausted her batteries. She saw the man rise to his feet. As if in slow motion she saw him raise the rifle to his shoulder. This time he was aiming straight at her. In that moment it occurred to her that Kobal had been right and she should never have left the safety of her prison. The world outside was her enemy and this was the assassin it had sent to kill her.

Then he fired — and the wolf that had been dragging its broken body towards her slumped dead at her side.

She saw the gun swing away from her . . . and followed the line of fire to the bear standing among the slaughtered wolves.

'No!' She was surprised at the power in her voice. It sounded as if it belonged to someone else.

The man lowered the rifle and looked at her, with his head to one side in a silent question.

'No,' she said, 'the bear's with me.'

She saw the look on his face and the absurdity of what she had said suddenly hit her.

'The bear's with me,' she said again and began to laugh hysterically, rolling over in the snow.

Then she saw the blood.

Strangely, it seemed to be coming from her.

She put her hand up to her neck and it was.

29

The Reindeer People

Her rescuer knelt beside her and gently pulled the blood-soaked material from her neck.

'How bad is it?' Jade said.

It felt very bad.

'You're going to be OK,' he said.

They always said that in all the war films she'd ever seen, even though everyone knew they were going to die.

In fact, they might as well say, 'I reckon you've got about ten seconds to live – any last words for your loved ones?'

She didn't have any last words. Except, perhaps, *sorry*.

Sorry for all the trouble I've caused. Sorry I missed

Christmas. Sorry I'll miss all the other Christmases.

'It's taken a sizeable hunk out of you,' he said, 'but nothing vital.'

Oh. So that was all right then.

He gave her a pad of lint to press on the wound while he rummaged in his first aid kit.

'I don't think it was the wolf,' he said, 'I think you just hit a rock when you fell. But I'll give you a tetanus shot just in case.'

Then she saw his arm.

His sleeve had been ripped to the elbow and she stared in horror at the exposed flesh of his arm: what there was of it. He had been savaged to the bone. His whole forearm was a mess of blood and torn sinew. It was a miracle he could move it.

'Who are you?' she said. Her mouth was so dry it came out as a croak.

'My name's Benedict,' he said. 'You, I suppose, are Jade.'

She wasn't quite sure she liked the way he said that.

'Why are you wearing a monk's robe?' he asked — as if there was nothing more important on his mind.

She didn't have the energy to tell him about it.

'Are you a doctor?' she said.

'No . . . but I'm good at mending things,' he told her, clamping the dressing on her neck. 'And I drove an ambulance during the . . .' He frowned. 'During a war.'

When he'd bandaged her up he left her for a moment to see to his friend. He came back looking grim.

'Is he going to be OK?' she said.

'He's in pretty bad shape. I think he's got a fractured skull. I'm going to have to get help.' He looked at her doubtfully. 'You'd better come with me.'

'I'll be all right,' she said. She didn't think she could walk another step. She inclined her head towards the bear. 'Laurie will look after me.'

'OK.' He nodded but he didn't look very happy. 'I'll be back within the hour.'

It was a very long hour.

She had begun to shake uncontrollably. The bear came and sat down beside her and she huddled close to him for comfort and warmth. There was a pale light in the clouds where the sun was trying to break through but she didn't give much for its chances. She wondered how long the remains of

289

the wolf pack would take to get back to Castle Piru and what Kobal would do next. He had plenty of choices and she knew he wouldn't give up trying to get her back.

She heard a noise. It was like a lawnmower. Several lawnmowers. Moments later three snowmobiles came roaring over the summit of the fell. She recognized Benedict on the first – the others were all men, all armed with rifles.

Two of the vehicles had trailers in tow and they put the shaman in one, Jade and the bear in the other. They clearly weren't very pleased about it but Jade was too tired to care. Within minutes of setting off she was asleep in the bear's lap.

She slept for the entire journey and only awoke when Benedict lifted her down from the trailer. There was a tremendous noise of barking dogs. It sounded like there were hundreds of them.

'Where are we?' she cried out in alarm, half expecting to see Kobal's pit bulls again . . . but they were huskies – sled dogs – driven into a frenzy by the bear. She could see reindeer too, in pens among the trees, and a good many of the cone-shaped tents the *Sami* called *karta*. They seemed to be a large camp along the side of a lake – not Lake Piru, she hoped.

She felt as if she was back in the game, when anything could happen.

'It's just a camp for the reindeer herders,' Benedict reassured her as he carried her through the snow and the mud. 'You'll be safe here.'

Unexpectedly she *felt* safe. For the first time in months. She looked down at his arm expecting to see it bandaged but it wasn't. The sleeve was hanging in shreds and there was dried blood all over it but no wound. Not even a scar.

'Who are you?' she said again. She looked up into his face and saw the likeness to Kobal and in her fear and confusion she thought it *was* him in some disguise or other – the blond, fair-haired version – and the whole episode had been one of his games after all – an elaborate trick.

'No,' he said, shaking his head. 'I'm not Kobal . . .' It was only later that she realized he'd read her thoughts.

'I'm his brother.'

30

The Nephilim

It was dark when she awoke. For a moment she thought she was back in the Castle of Demons and the events of the past twenty-four hours were like a dream – or a version of the game. She stared into the darkness, waiting for Kobal to lift the black helmet from her head. She put her hand up to feel for it – but all she felt was hair, matted with dried blood, and the dressing on her neck.

She raised herself on one elbow and looked about her. There was a fire in the centre of the room and by the light of the glowing embers she saw that she was in one of the *karta* – the tents of the reindeer people. Benedict must have brought her here. But how long ago? She still had her watch on. Two-thirty. She had slept for over twelve hours. She felt all the better for it but anxious too. She made a mental list of all the things she was anxious about. It was a long one. Beginning with . . .

Benedict was Kobal's *brother*?

Did he mean his *real* brother?

She hadn't had a chance to pursue the question when they arrived at the camp. He had been desperate to get his friend off to hospital and she'd been too weary to think straight. She'd made him promise to look after Laurie, who needed attention to several small wounds. Then she'd collapsed on the mattress provided for her in the *karta*.

It was possible of course that he just meant brother in the broader sense – 'he's my bro' – or even the religious sense – as in monk or friar. But she didn't think so. He meant brother as in brother. As in kin. And this stirred a distant memory. Something Kobal had told her several months ago when they were still in England. A story about his brother who had a split-personality disorder – schizophrenia – and was all the things her Aunt Em had said Kobal was: *mad, bad and dangerous to know*.

So who was she to believe?

Another thought occurred to her. If Benedict *was*

Kobal's brother, that made him her uncle.

Another member of the family. Another skeleton in the cupboard.

It was starting to get quite crowded in there.

And thinking about skeletons made her think about Benedict's arm and the miraculous way it had healed.

I've always been good at mending things . . .

She deserved some answers . . . but they would have to wait until morning. All this thinking had made her feel extremely weary again. She turned over on her side, away from the light of the fire, and within seconds she had slipped back into a dreamless sleep.

When next she awoke it was daylight and Benedict was standing there with breakfast on a tray. She must have smelled it. A whole stack of pancakes with berries and cream. She hadn't eaten for two days.

But then a flood of memories came surging back.

'What's happening?' she asked as she struggled to sit up. She felt as if she'd been kicked all over.

'Nothing much,' he assured her as he set the tray down next to her bed. 'But the sun's shining and Jussa

Proksi's on the mend and you're still alive – so let's count our blessings.'

'Just what?

'Jussa Proksi. The shaman. My friend. He got a bad knock on the head but he's out of danger.'

'And Laurie?'

'Laurie?'

'My bear?'

'Oh, he's yours, is he? We were wondering what to do with him. He's all right. I took this out of him.'

He took a small piece of cloth from his pocket and opened it out very carefully on the palm of his hand to reveal what looked like a small flat piece of plastic.

'What is it?' She peered at it, mystified.

'It's a computer chip. He kept scratching his head and I felt it just under the skin. It's how Kobal controlled him.'

'I don't understand . . .'

'Nor do I. Not entirely. It's some of Kobal's devilry. He probably finds it a lot easier than training them.'

'Training what?'

'Bears. And whatever else he's got in his bestiary.'

'So – he's a *real* bear?'

'Of course.' Now *he* looked mystified. 'What did you think he was – a rug?'

'I thought . . . I thought he was some kind of robot,' she said. She felt foolish suddenly.

'Well, he is – or was – with this in him. It had stopped working though. I mean, it was no longer receiving signals. Lucky for you. Or Kobal would probably have got him to bring you back.'

'It must've been the electric shocks,' she concluded thoughtfully.

'Excuse me?'

'Kobal made us give him electric shocks.'

He frowned.

'Not that I did, of course,' she added hastily.

'But the others did?'

She nodded grimly. 'Kobal said he couldn't feel anything – but he can, can't he?' For the first time she really began to hate her father. 'Why doesn't anyone ever tell me the truth?' she demanded.

He regarded her curiously. 'You mean Kobal?'

'I mean Kobal, my parents – that is the people I *thought* were my parents – my Aunt Em, *you*.'

'Me? When have I ever lied to you?'

'I don't know,' she admitted grudgingly. 'I haven't caught you out yet.'

He laughed. 'That's a relief.' Then he saw her face. 'Sorry.'

She pointed accusingly. 'What happened to your arm?'

He raised both arms and looked down at them as if puzzled. He was all cleaned up and wearing a pale-blue fleece.

'What arm?' he said.

She'd forgotten which one it was now.

'The one the wolf had in its mouth.' Her voice rose in exasperation. 'It was all crunched up, down to the bone and I saw it a few minutes later and there was nothing wrong with it.'

'I heal easily,' he said.

'There you are,' she exclaimed triumphantly. 'No one ever gives me a straight answer.'

She made a start on her breakfast.

'But it *is* a straight answer. I do heal easily. It's some genetic thing. I'm a freak.'

'You and me both,' she muttered as she heaped berries on her plate.

He regarded her with amusement.

'I'm sorry,' he said. 'You've had a rough time, haven't you?'

'I wouldn't mind,' she said through a mouthful of pancake, 'if people were straight with me.'

He sat down at the end of the bed.

'OK. So what do you want to know?'

'How come you and Kobal are brothers?'

'Er . . . we had the same father and mother . . .?'

'Yeah, right . . .' She was about to make some cutting remark about people hating a smartypants – the way they did to her – when another thought struck her. 'Are they still alive?'

'Who?' he said.

'Your parents.'

More relatives. She could have a pair of grandparents somewhere – and who knows what else?

But he shook his head. 'They died a long time ago,' he said.

'How?'

Later, she wondered about that *how*. As if it mattered *how* they had died. Perhaps she already had her suspicions, festering in the darkness of her mind.

But it was a key question. It opened the family cupboard . . .

And the skeletons came tumbling out.

'My mother was burned as a witch,' he told her, 'and my father was garrotted. Strangled from behind,' he explained, in case she wasn't familiar with the process, 'with a thin cord. Then he had a stake driven through his heart.'

'Right.' She thought of telling him it wasn't very nice to joke about his parents like that. But he didn't look as if he was joking. 'When was this – the Middle Ages?'

'As a matter of fact it was. My father died on the tenth of October 1225, and my mother two days later.'

She stared at him. 'You're kidding me – right?' But she felt a shiver run up her spine.

'Is this the kind of thing you kid about?' he asked her curiously, as if he really wanted to know.

'No, but I mean if your mother died in . . . I mean . . .' She laughed nervously. 'You'd be . . .?'

'Seven hundred and eighty-three,' he said, 'on my next birthday.'

'That's ridiculous,' she said.

'It is,' he agreed. 'Totally ridiculous. I stopped celebrating after the first hundred.'

She considered him carefully.

'You're not kidding me, are you?'

'No,' he said.

It would explain the wound thing. Well, not *explain* it but . . . She shook her head in bewilderment. 'So – where is all this supposed to have happened? Burning witches and what d'you call it?'

'Garrotting. In Transylvania. Kolozsvar, to be precise. At least that's what the Hungarians called it then. We called it Klausenburg.'

'Transylvania?' Another shiver of alarm — or premonition. 'Where the vampires come from?'

'Yes. Interestingly the legend of the vampires seems to have begun around this time. I think we probably got the blame for it.'

' "We". . .? Who's "we"?'

'The Saviour Knights. We were working for the King of Hungary at the time — fighting the pagans in Transylvania. As you do. Well, as you did then — if you were a Crusader.'

'Hang on.' She put her hand to her head. She was beginning to get one of her migraines. 'The *what* Knights?'

'The Knights of the Order of Saint Saviour of Antioch. That's the official title. The Hungarians called us the Nephilim. Ruder things, too, I'm afraid, at times, but—'

'The Nephilim?'

'After the sons of angels and the beautiful daughters of man.'

She nodded as if this made perfect sense.

'You don't know the story? It's in the Bible.'

'Oh well then,' she said. She considered another pancake but changed her mind. She'd lost her appetite a bit.

'Genesis chapter six, verses one to four,' he said as if she was going to challenge him on the subject. 'There are other references but that's the first. They tell of a gang of fallen angels who fell in love with the beautiful daughters of Seth – Adam's son – and made them pregnant. So the children were half angels. In some versions of the story they grew to be giants. In other versions God sends the flood as punishment to wipe them all out.'

'So you're not one of them?' It was worth asking.

'No, I'm not one of them. As far as I know. But the Knights of the Order, many of them came from Germany and Scandinavia and they were tall and blond so the Hungarians called them the Nephilim. My father was a Knight Commander – one of the leaders – but he disgraced himself. He fell in love with a Romanian woman who was accused of witchcraft.' He considered. 'She probably *was* a witch, in fact. The Knights were sworn to chastity but Conrad – that's my father – broke his vows and the woman became pregnant. She had twins.'

'You and Kobal?'

'He was christened Boris. We were taken from her of course – and a few days later they burned her.'

He was so matter-of-fact about it.

'They burned her? When she'd just had twins?'

As if it made it worse somehow.

'That was the punishment. She was accused of sorcery and black magic.'

'And what happened to you and – and your brother?'

'We were split up. I was sent to England; Boris to Germany. They thought we were the Devil's spawn. It wasn't safe to keep us together. Some would have had us killed. Drowned or strangled. But instead we were brought up by the holy Brothers – in strict discipline. A bit too strict, I suspect, in my brother's case. When we were old enough we both became Knights of the Order.' He shrugged. 'I still am, but Boris – he broke away and . . . became Kobal.'

She shook her head again. 'It's impossible.'

'Impossible,' he agreed. 'And yet we're living proof of it.' He sighed. 'I can't explain it to you – or to myself. Science would say we were . . . deviants. Produced by some kind of mutant gene. But I'm not a geneticist like your Aunt Em. I'm a child of the Middle Ages when science was regarded as sorcery.

We'd find a more supernatural explanation for the mysteries of life – and death.'

'But . . .' For once she was at a loss for words. 'What does it mean?'

'It means we don't age. Or at least we age very slowly. We don't get sick. And if we're wounded we heal very quickly. As you've noticed.'

'So – you can live for ever?'

'That's a good question. I don't know. I expect if you put a bomb under us we'd have a bit of a problem. If we were blown to atoms. And there are the usual superstitions. You know. That we can be killed by a silver bullet or by a stake through the heart – like vampires. The Undead. Or by one of our own kind. Perhaps that's what will happen. Perhaps I'll be killed by Kobal – or he by me. Or perhaps we'll kill ourselves.'

'Could you? Kill yourself?'

'I suppose so. Suicide would count as being killed by one's own kind, wouldn't it?'

'I mean would you want to?'

'I can't say I haven't thought about it. Life can become tiresome if you live for eighty years – think what it's like when you've lived for eight hundred, near enough. There's no sense of . . . completion.'

'But to die . . .?'

'Isn't always such a terrible thing. If you've lived a good life. Would *you* want to live for ever?'

'I don't know.' She put a hand up to the dressing on her neck. 'Doesn't everyone? Perhaps not . . . for ever.'

He leaned over. 'Let me take a look at that.' He lifted up a corner of the dressing, very gently so it didn't hurt her, and peered at the wound. 'It's coming along but it hasn't healed like . . . magic. I don't think you're going to live for ever. If you were hurt badly, you would die I think.' He smiled cheerfully. 'So don't take any chances.'

Then, as he replaced the dressing, he continued in a more thoughtful tone. 'There was once a man called Origen. A Greek philosopher, one of the early fathers of the Christian Church. He believed that the soul strives for perfection: to be reunited with God, its creator. That men and women have the capacity to become perfect beings – angels if you like. And even the fallen angels are not beyond redemption. Even the Devil himself.'

'That's . . . quite good, isn't it?'

'I think so. Unfortunately others didn't. He was condemned by the Church as a heretic and tortured to death. But I've always though it was an admirable philosophy. I would like to "move on", I think. Provided of course it's a promotion.' He grinned. 'Have you had enough breakfast? I'll take the tray.'

But she wasn't finished with him yet.

'How did you and Kobal come to be so different?'

If they *were* different. She wasn't sure about that yet.

'Oh, lots of reasons. We weren't brought up together but we both suffered as children, in different ways. And Boris – Kobal – may have suffered more. Certainly he reacted to it differently.'

'Which of you is the oldest?'

'Me. By about two hours. And he has never forgiven me for it.'

'Why not?'

'Because I was the first. And for two hours – or at least part of that time – my mother, *our* mother, held me in her arms.'

'How do you know?'

'I know,' he said simply. 'What I don't know is why they didn't take me away from her. Maybe they were afraid to. In case she cursed them. But by the time Kobal was born she was exhausted and they took us both away. He never felt his mother's arms around him.'

And nor had Jade.

'Is that why he turned out to be . . . the way he is?'

'Oh I don't know. I don't think it helped. Why does anyone turn out the way they do? But in the final resort, it's down to you. You either choose the light or the dark. And Boris, he chose the dark.'

'And I'm his daughter,' she said bitterly.

He looked at her sharply. 'We don't know that – not for sure. He's a terrible liar and besides, I was always under the impression that we couldn't have children.'

For a moment she felt a tremendous relief. But then . . .

'If he's not my father, then who is?'

'Does that matter very much to you?'

'Of course it matters.'

'Why?'

'Well . . . because . . .' She had to think about it. 'Because if you don't know who your father or your mother are – how can you know who *you* are?'

He considered this as if it were an interesting question that had never occurred to him before.

'Well, I suppose it's the things you care about, the

friends you make, the choices . . . Yes,' he nodded as if he'd come to a conclusion, 'it's the choices you make that make you what you are. As much as anything.'

'I'm like him – a bit.' She had never thought she would ever admit to that but it was true. And Benedict was like him too – in some ways. This must mean something. 'I can read people's thoughts. I know what makes them frightened and –' she swallowed hard '– and I can use it against them.'

'I know that,' he said gently. 'But even if it's true and Kobal *is* your father – it doesn't mean you have to be like him. You have a choice,' he repeated firmly. 'We all have a choice. The great wizard Merlin was said to be a child of the Devil but he did some good, I think.'

'I like having power,' she said doubtfully. 'Is that bad?'

'It can be. It depends how you use it.'

'Sometimes, though, I just want to be ordinary.'

He threw back his head then and laughed as if this was really funny.

'You and me both,' he said.

31

The Gates of Hell

All through the daylight hours they came in: grim-faced men driving SUVs and pick-ups and carrying guns. They came from the surrounding villages and farms and from the more remote parts of Lapland – some from Sweden and Norway and Russia, even – in answer to the call.

The *Sami* were preparing for war.

'They're going to attack the castle.' Benedict said. He didn't sound too pleased about it. 'With Jussa Proksi gone there's no holding them back. They mean to release the prisoners and burn the place to the ground.'

'The prisoners?' Jade frowned. Did he mean the children? Apparently not.

x

'Several of the herdsmen have gone missing since Kobal turned up in the area and they reckon he's holding them there, against their will.'

'I saw one of them. In the dungeons. At least, it might have been.' She told him about the man she had seen, if it *was* a man. 'He was like a wild animal. Worse.'

Benedict nodded grimly. 'It's possible Kobal has been experimenting on them, to turn them into his creatures, like your bear.'

She shuddered. Maybe she had been lucky. Or maybe the mind games he had played on her were more subtle, more dangerous, than planting a computer chip in her brain.

'But what about the other kids?' she said.

'That's what I'm worried about. If I don't get to them before the *Sami* do.'

'You're going in with them?'

'Of course.' He seemed surprised she should ask.

'Let me go with you,' she said impulsively.

'You? You'd go back, into that? Why?'

'Because – I don't know, I suppose because I helped bring them there. I can't just abandon them.'

She wasn't that fond of her half-brothers and sisters, especially after the business with Laurie, but she felt responsible for them. And besides she didn't want them burned to death. Not even Paco, the Child of Fire.

But Benedict was shaking his head. 'It's too dangerous. And I promised to keep you safe.'

'Promised who?'

'Your Aunt Em. I've just been speaking to her on the phone. She's flying out from England to pick you up.'

England. Just like that. Flying out from England to pick her up. And it would all be over.

But it couldn't be. Not like that.

'I can help,' she insisted. 'I know my way around the place.'

'Well, it would be a help if you could draw a map,' he said.

He brought pencil and paper and she drew a cross-section of the castle as well as she could remember it.

'The main gate is over the bridge,' she told him. 'But there's another, a small one, just here . . .' She marked the spot where she'd escaped with Laurie. 'It leads into a small courtyard and there's another door leading into the castle just here. With a spiral staircase going up and down. The kids are on the fourth floor where I was. Down the stairs is the motor museum and the dungeons.'

'The *motor museum*?'

She told him about the killer cars in the basement – and the Zeppelin.

'*A Zeppelin?*' He shook his head. 'I knew he was crazy – but a *Zeppelin*?'

'Only a small one. He called it a prototype for the ones that bombed London.'

'Well, let's be grateful for small mercies. How did he get it in there?'

'What do you mean?'

'Well, I presume there has to be a way of getting these things into the place – and out.'

'Oh yes, there was a ramp, leading up. The whole place is a maze,' she said, by way of explanation. 'It's hard to explain but it's like it's bigger on the inside than on the outside. Like a House of Mirrors at a funfair.'

'A House of Mirrors.' He nodded as if this made sense. 'That would figure.'

'Sorry?'

'I've always thought of Hell as a House of Mirrors, sort of. Distorting mirrors, going on for ever.' He seemed to have gone off into some world of his own but then he saw her watching him. He smiled as if at his own foolish fantasies. 'Back in the Middle Ages, when people were wiser, or crazier, than they are now, there was a widespread belief in Hell – as a real place, where the Demons and the Damned were condemned to spend the whole of eternity. And for some reason, people believed the entrance to Hell was in Lapland. Perhaps because it's so remote. According to *Sami* legend, the Gates of Hell were on an island on Lake Piru, the Lake of Demons. Where the castle is now.'

'Do you believe that?'

'I believe there is more to Castle Piru than meets the eye. As you've just told me. Some secret, in the heart of the labyrinth, that only Kobal knows about. The *Sami* believe he's creating his own demons there. But I think he has other plans.' He shrugged. 'Well, we'll know soon enough.'

'I've got to come with you,' she insisted. 'You can't leave me out of it. Not after all I've been through. I can help you, honest I can.'

He shook his head but she knew he was weakening.

'The *Sami* don't know what they're up against,' he said. 'He'll turn their minds to jelly. They'll end up shooting each other.'

She knew he was right. She had some of that power herself.

'That's why I have to go with them,' he said. 'I have to block him.'

'Can you do that?'

'Yes. I think so. Or at least, I can distract him. But if I do – and the *Sami* get into the castle and slaughter the kids . . .'

'Can't you stop them?'

'I don't know. I'll need all my energy – and concentration – for Kobal. Bit of a problem.' He smiled ruefully.

'I could look after the kids.'

He regarded her thoughtfully. 'Is there anywhere safe they could go? In the castle? Until I can get to them.'

She thought. Somewhere safe – in that place? Then she remembered.

'The tank!'

'The tank?'

'There's an old Russian tank – in the motor museum. If they could get inside . . .'

She saw that she had caught his interest.

'Is there one of them you could . . . "communicate" with?'

'Sure. Any of them.'

'We need one the others would follow. Without question.'

'Paco.' Her face fell.

He looked at her enquiringly. 'You having doubts?'

'No. I can do it.'

'Right,' he said. 'This is the deal. You stick by me. You don't go anywhere without me. And while I'm concentrating on Kobal, you concentrate on this Paco. OK?'

She nodded. 'OK.'

'Then you'd better get some sleep,' he said. 'We attack at dawn.'

32

The Siege of Castle Piru

They came out on the lake, by the ruined shelter where she had stopped with Laurie, shortly after their escape. She could see the castle clearly across the water, the tops of its turrets catching the light of the rising sun.

'This was where they kept watch,' said Benedict looking around the ruin.

'Who?' asked Jade vaguely; she was still watching the castle.

'The men from the village. They were supposed to keep an eye on the place – and you. But clearly someone was keeping an eye on *them*. Two of them were killed here over a month ago and no one's been back since.'

It brought back a distant memory, of a morning in winter when she had walked on the battlements with Laurie and the snow was falling.

'I felt I was being watched,' she said. 'I felt . . . in danger.'

But not as much as she did now. She looked back towards the castle as the sunlight slowly advanced down the grim walls. She imagined Kobal waking up and looking out and seeing her standing there and his eyes burning into her: the traitor, the daughter who had betrayed him.

And would he see the men, creeping through the forest, with their guns and their grenades? Hundreds of them, all trained soldiers in the Finnish Defence Force.

But she had seen Kobal in action and she knew they had no chance. He would turn them against each other or scare the daylights out of them and send them running terrified through the forest, clawing at the nightmares he had put into their heads.

Unless Benedict could stop him.

She looked at him now. He had dressed in a black tunic, belted at the waist, with a white cross on the front, like a Crusader knight, and he was carrying a sword that was too heavy for her to lift. He stood on the edge of the lake and placed the point on the ground and folded both hands around the hilt and stood there looking out over the still waters towards the Castle of Demons.

What are you like, she thought.

She knew the answer to that one. He was like Kobal.

'It helps me concentrate,' he said.

'Whatever,' she muttered under her breath.

Then a movement caught her eye, high on the castle walls, as high as you could go. A figure in black.

Kobal.

It had to be. And there was a flash of light as the sun was reflected on something bright. A sword, like Benedict's? It would not have surprised her.

Benedict had seen him too. He pushed the hilt of the sword away from his body and stood there, braced at the side of the lake, as if he was at the helm of a ship heading into the eye of the storm.

She knew the conflict had begun.

But she had her own problems.

Or to be more specific. Paco.

She sat cross-legged on the ground beside the motionless figure of the warrior monk and tried to concentrate.

There was a sudden burst of rifle fire. The *Sami* had begun their attack. She tried to put this out of her mind and focus on the image of Paco.

Where are you?

She stared at a patch of water, at the edge of the lake. Dark water, still in shadow, deep and dark . . .

Where are you, you little horror?

Come out, come out, wherever you are . . .

Fire. A ring of fire on the water. Impossible – but the water was burning. A finger of flame reached towards her.

And she was burning.

Tied to a stake like a witch, the witch-mother of Benedict and Kobal, and the flames engulfing her. She could barely see for the smoke. Her body was on fire.

She fought the flames grimly. Shook herself clear of the image of the witch and focused on herself, who she really was.

But who *was* she?

The Child of the Forest.

And at once she saw it in her mind's eye. The Forest of Windsor where she had been born. The old forest of the distant past, a forest of mighty oaks, stretching into the haze.

But it was a haze of smoke. The forest was burning. And again she felt the heat rising towards her, burning into her mind.

She was the Child of the Forest but the forest could not fight fire. And Paco was the Child of Fire.

And this time she saw him. A face in the flames, smiling a cruel smile of victory.

'*No.*' She snarled the word through gritted teeth.

She was the Child of the Forest but she was also the Child of Earth.

Earth. She focused on the Earth.

She saw an empty desert, baking in the heat of the sun. Parched and lifeless. The Earth after the Apocalypse. The time of the heat.

No. Again. Fight it.

Something scuttling among the rocks. A scorpion. The scorpion trapped in a circle of flame, stinging itself to death.

No. Not the scorpion. The rocks. Think of the rocks.

She was a rock. A mighty rock. Rising out of the desert. Timeless, enduring, stronger than wind or rain or sun . . .

The shape of Angel Rock formed in her mind and she held on to it grimly as the flames burned into her.

But flames held no power over rock.

They were dying, burning out and she was untouched.

And now she saw his face again.

Not smiling now. But angry – and fearful.

Where are you? she said again, and she sent her mind charging across the lake and through the castle walls and she found him at last, cowering now on the floor of his room, beneath the window.

Paco, you little beast, what are you scared of? Vultures, rats, dogs . . . No. Me?

I'm scarier than all of them put together, Paco. El Jefe. *Chief of the Lost Children. I can crush you into dust. I can bury you under a mountain of rubbish, like the one I found you in . . .*

But no. This was not the way.

You are here to save him, not destroy him.

To save him and the others.

What does he care about?

Survival. Yes. Whatever else he is, Paco is a survivor.

So tell him how to survive. So long as he takes the others with him.

You will *take the others with you, Paco. Or you will answer to me. Do you understand?*

He nodded.

So she told him about the tank.

He understood. He ran from room to room collecting his little band of followers and leading them down the spiral stairs towards the basement and the Museum of Killer Cars.

And Jade was with them, shepherding them to safety.

She could see the stairs, winding down into darkness.

But then something happened.

The darkness was rising towards her, coming up to meet her.

She fought it but she could feel the darkness rising and the panic with it, just as the flames had risen but much more frightening. Darkness so complete it drained her of all feeling, all sense of self. She was drowning in darkness. And there was nothing of her left.

33

The Zeppelin

A light through the trees. Sunlight sparkling on the surface of the water. A cool hand on her brow.

She was lying by the side of the lake and Benedict was kneeling beside her, raising her from the ground and stroking the hair back from her forehead.

'It's all right,' he murmured softly. 'It's all right. You're out of it. You're safe.'

She felt the panic again.

'Where are they? I lost them.'

'It's all right,' he said again. 'You couldn't help it.'

'But what happened?'

'Kobal. He broke off the fight with me – and turned on you. And you can't fight Kobal. Not yet.'

'But what happened to the . . .'

She struggled up to a sitting position and looked out over the lake.

The castle was on fire. She saw flames in the windows and the smoke rising into the pale blue sky . . . But there was something else, something more tangible than smoke . . .

A long, fat cigar-shape, rising from the castle walls, rising through the smoke . . .

The Zeppelin.

Benedict was watching it too, his face grim.

'Kobal?' she said.

He nodded.

'He's escaping?'

'Yes.'

'Can't you stop him? Can't you bring it down?'

'No. He's got the children with him.'

And they both watched helplessly as the Zeppelin turned into the rising sun and made its stately way through the burning sky towards Russia.

34

Choices

A dark cloud lay over the eastern end of the lake. Jade would have taken it for a storm cloud had she not known it was the smoke from the burning castle.

It seemed like a brooding presence and she half expected Kobal to come flying out of it on his Zeppelin to claim her for his own. His missing child.

'So he's gone,' she said flatly. 'And taken them with him.'

'Well, at least they're safe. For the time being,' said Benedict. 'At least we achieved that much.'

She looked back towards the castle, still burning through the smoke. All of it gone. The flamingos and the fruit bat, all the other weird creatures Kobal had created, the computers and the killer cars, the costumes and the props of his mad existence . . . All that magic gone, all gone in a pyre of smoke.

And Kobal too.

'He's got to come down somewhere,' said Benedict. 'And the Russians don't like people flying over their borders without permission. Even in an old German Zeppelin.'

'What will they do to him?'

'Stick him in prison for a long time. Or hand him back to the British. Or the Americans. Or whoever else wants him for whatever crimes he's committed.'

'And the children?'

'Will be taken into care. Or sent back where they came from.'

'Like me?'

Her Aunt Em would be arriving before nightfall. By special helicopter from Kittila.

'Isn't that what you want? To go back home? To get back to normal?'

Home. Normal. They sounded so strange to her now, so distant, after what she had been through.

'I just want to be ordinary,' she had said to Benedict, only the day before yesterday. But was she sure about that?

'What about you?' she asked him.

'Me? I'll just go on being me. I don't have much choice.' He seemed sad about it.

'Will I see you again?'

'Do you want to?'

'You're my uncle,' she reminded him. 'You're the closest family I've got – after Kobal.'

If he was telling the truth. For once.

'Well, I guess we'll just have to look out for each other,' he said.

'Yes. I'd like that.'

At least, she'd like him looking out for her.

'What do *you* think I should do?' she asked him.

He considered her carefully.

'I think you should go back with your Aunt Em. Go back to school. Get on with the business of growing up. It's complicated enough, without worrying about anything else.'

'And what about – being different?'

'Oh, everybody is different, in their own way. You just have to deal with it. And make the best of it. Not the worst.'

'You know what I mean. I can read people's minds. I can put thoughts in their heads, terrible thoughts.'

'Only if you want to.'

He was right. She didn't *have* to be different.

'There's worse things than being ordinary,' he said.

'Like what?'

'Like having power. And using it. Like Kobal does.'

'OK,' she said. 'I'll give it a go.'

'Good. That's one decision made. And now – what are you going to do about the bear?'

'Me?'

'You brought him here. He's your responsibility.'

'Is it always like this? All these decisions?'

He grinned. 'Fraid so.'

'Can we set him free? I mean, really free. In the forest.'

'I don't see why not. It's where he came from.'

'OK. Let's do it.'

And then she shivered. Because she heard Kobal's voice in her own.

They drove out from the camp in a pick-up with Laurie chained in the back. Jade didn't like the idea of the chain but he was restive – wholly changed from the bear she had known in Castle Piru, even on the fells: much more of a wild thing – and there was a danger, Benedict said, that he would jump out and hurt himself while they were on the way.

They drove for about an hour along a track beside the lake and then turned off into the forest.

Spring was come at last to Lapland, the true spring. The sun shone from a cloudless sky, the snows had retreated to the summits of the distant fells and the first flowers had appeared on the forest floor. Benedict told her the names of some of them; flowers Jade had never heard of, much less seen: the purple saxifrage, the purplish-red crowberry and the flowering cotton grass known as hare's tail – yellow with a little button of black in the centre where it had pushed up through the frozen peat . . . When they stopped the car they could hear birdsong – the cheerful notes of a chaffinch and the chuckle of black grouse in the distance – and then the sudden, startling cry of a raven.

Benedict released the bear from the back and passed one end of the chain to Jade.

'Over to you,' he said. But he watched carefully as the bear scrambled down to the ground – and he had his rifle ready.

They had put a quick-release catch on the collar at his neck and Jade pulled it back and lifted it free.

The bear looked at her. Was there a glimmer of recognition there? It was hard to tell.

'Go on, Laurie,' she said, pointing into the forest. 'You're free to go.'

He raised himself on to his hind legs and growled – and it took all her courage not to jump back. He looked down at her from his great height and it was as if he was trying to fix her in his memory – but she knew this was a childish fancy – then he dropped to all fours again and ran in that shambling, clownish was he had into the forest.

He didn't look back.

She heard Kobal's voice again, in her head.

Don't look back. Move on. Never look back.

'Good,' said Benedict. 'That was a good thing to do.'

'Yes,' she said with a sigh.

'You gave him his freedom.'

'Yes,' said Jade again, and she was happy about that. Now all she had to do was find her own.

Above the songs of the birds and the sighing of the wind in the trees she heard something else. Something harsh and alien. It grew louder. She looked up and there in the sky above the forest she saw the helicopter – the helicopter bringing her Aunt Em up from Kittila, to take her home.

Acknowledgments

I'd like to thank the many people who have helped me with the research and writing for the *Mysteries of the Septagram* series, in particular: Philip Holmes and the staff of the Esther Benjamini Trust for their work among circus children in India; Dermot Bryers and Marta Calvo and the other volunteers from Oxford University who spend their summers working with the children of the rubbish dumps of Guatemala City; Bibi Baskin and the staff of the Raheem Residency in Alleppey, Kerrala, who provided me such a wonderful workplace on the shores of the Arabian Sea; the teachers and children of Belleville, Fircroft, Graveney and Crofton schools in south London for the focus groups they kindly arranged for me; to the Sami families in the Kittila and Inari areas of Lapland who housed me, fed me, found me when I got lost and taught me all I needed to know about demons and huskies (which are sometimes interchangeable), and most of all to Rosemary Canter of United Agents and Beverley Birch at Hachette for helping me to turn it all into a book.

Read on for more adventure in the next
Mysteries of the Septagram
ABYSS
Coming soon . . .

She exploded into a world of sound and storm and furious swirling water – and an intense biting cold, a cold that seemed to make the inside of the car at the bottom of a river seem almost cosy.

And a blazing light that hit her right in the face, dazzling her.

The light was a surprise. She had not expected the light. It was a flashlight, she realized – in the brief moment before other concerns wiped it from her mind – a flashlight sweeping the surface of the water. She did not see the figure, or figures behind it but she knew they must be from the other car. Barmella, perhaps, or even Kobal himself. This was not something she was allowed to dwell upon, for the river was in flood, a raging torrent fed by a thousand others swollen by rainwater pouring off the surrounding hills. It had burst its banks, rising almost to the arch of the bridge and sweeping all before it in its headlong rush to the sea: branches, whole trees even, lengths of fencing, sheds, dead sheep, flotsam and jetsam of every description – and Jade.

She was swept away at a rate of knots, leaving the flashlight, the car, the bridge far behind her: a blur of images engraved on her mind before the darkness swallowed them up and she was fighting for her life.

She was a good swimmer. A school champion. But that was in a swimming pool. This was different. You couldn't swim in this. You certainly couldn't swim *against* it. You were just one more piece of debris caught up in the flood. You just went with the flow and tried to keep your head above the water.

And oh, it was cold. So cold she wanted to give up, to surrender to it, to sink into the illusory warmth of death.

And where was Aunt Em? Was she dead already, or fighting for her own life just a few feet away? Jade cried out to her in the darkness but there was no answering cry and she could not have heard it if there was.

Something crashed into her, knocking what little breath she had left in her body but somehow she managed to cling to it. A tree, or a large branch. She pulled herself a little out of the water and searched for another bobbing head but it was impossible to see anything in that relentless surge. It was like a great black-backed beast, a wild thing, a monstrous serpent surging through the night. And so cold. Deathly cold. One shivering misery of cold. If she let go she would sink and it would be all over. There was a warm fire waiting for her . . . Only let go.

No, another voice commanded sternly. *Cling on, cling on, for dear life.*

A great crash. Her life-raft had hit one of the trees that lined the banks, the former banks, now deep in water. Another crash and she screamed and almost lost her grip. It was a bend in the river. And the bank was high at this point, a rocky crag, a cliff almost, rising above her against the night sky with a cluster of trees at its foot and the rushing waters surging around them. Crash! Another tree. And this time she lost her precious hold. The waters closed over her head. She surfaced, gasping and choking, and went down again, down for the last time . . . except that her groping fingers found a trailing root and held on, knowing it was her last chance of life, the river pulling at her like a live thing . . . And was swept round like a limp rag and dumped into a backwater in the lee of a rocky outcrop, a miraculous haven from the monster's fury.

She dragged herself up on to the slippery surface of the rock. Rain and spray lashed her face and the river surged at her feet, threatening to hurl her back into its clutches. But there was a tree rising above her, sticking out from the very base of the cliff, just clear of the floodwater . . . She took a few tottering steps and clung to it for dear life.

At last she felt safe from the river, but she could not stay here. She was shivering uncontrollably. She would freeze to death in a matter of minutes. She looked up at the cliff above. Impossible. But she had to try. She had to find shelter or die. She forced herself to concentrate, to look for some means of climbing that towering cliff. And yet it wasn't so very high – no more than thirty or forty feet perhaps – and there were more trees growing out from the side, out over the river, their roots clinging to the soil and rock, the trunks projecting outwards at an angle.

She began to drag herself up by root and branch, her feet sliding from under her on the slippery slope, stones and muck dropping into the river below, rain and mud sluicing down on her. Several times she slid back but managed to grab a hold before she plunged to her death – for she would die, she knew, if she fell into that river again. It was like some deadly game of snakes and ladders. But she was so tired. She had to rest. She made it to the next tree, the last tree, the river below like a pit filled with angry writhing serpents hissing and roaring for her, their vanished prey, almost hypnotizing her to let go and drop back into their greedy jaws. She looked up. She could see the top of the cliff now just three or four metres above her head. But they were three or four metres of sheer rock, slick with rain. There were no more trees, no more ladders . . .

She could not have come so far only to be cheated now. She stood up with her back against the tree feeling the rain on her face, the rain and the tears.

'Help me, please help me,' she begged. Help me, she prayed to the nuns of Saint Severa's and the God they served. Help me, she prayed to Benedict, the warrior monk who might be her uncle. But she didn't pray to Kobal, who was her father. She didn't pray to him. She was not so desperate she would pray to him. She would rather slide back into the terrible river than pray to him.

And then she saw the bough.

It was just above her head, growing at a sharp angle toward the top of the cliff.

She turned very carefully, shuffling her feet round

one after the other until she was facing the tree. Her cheek was pressed agianst the wet bark, her arms wrapped around the trunk as if she was hugging it. She groped around in the darkness for a handhold. Nothing. But then as she stretched her hands up as far as she could on either side of the tree she found something. A knobbly knot of wood, a little above her head. Not much of a hold but enough, if she had the strength – and the courage. She clawed her fingers into the wood and heaved, pulling herself inch by inch up the greasy pole, reaching with her left hand for the branch just a few tantalizing inches higher. If she slipped now nothing would save her. But then her fingers closed round the precious lifeline and she hung on with her left hand, almost pulling her shoulder out at the socket and made a grab with the right. Now she was hanging from the bough with both arms. All she had to do was pull herself up. Barmella had made her do chin ups often enough in the gym in the Castle of Demons. She could still hear that fiendish voice driving her on.

'*Von more, only von. Vone more. You can do it!*'

She'd managed twelve at the last count.

She heaved, scrabbling with her feet against the tree trunk until she was hanging upside down like a sloth. One more effort. *Just von more.* She managed to throw one leg over, then an arm. Now her whole body. Yes! Panting with exhaustion, lying full length along the branch. Less like a slimy sloth now, more like a leopard. *Thank you, Barmella. Did you know that all those work outs were for this, so I could escape from you?*

But now what?

She knew now what. She had to crawl up that sloping, slender limb towrds the top of the ridge. With nothing beneath her but the river and the rocks.

But she couldn't. She wasn't a leopard. Or even a sloth.

There were only two ways of doing this. She either had to sit astride it and shuffle along on her bottom – or she had to stand up and walk along it.

She knew that was the best way but she dreaded it. She wasn't an acrobat either.

She eased herself up so she was standing with her back against the trunk and the branch arching away towards the top of the cliff. She could just see the clumps of grass at the edge. And beyond to the open countryside and the dark humps of the sleeping fells in the distance, darker even than the sky. Not a light, no sign of shelter, as far as she could see.

But she would worry about that later. She reached

out a foot, still supporting herself with one hand against the tree trunk.

But she couldn't do it. Not like this she couldn't. She had to take a run at it. Two steps and a jump.

She froze with horror at the thought. She was shivering again, her whole body wracked with shuddering sobs and her teeth like piano keys beating a frantic tuneless dirge, a funeral dirge. She forced herself to be still, conjured up an image of herself soaring through the air to safety.

OK, let's do it!

One, two . . . and a great scream as her foot slipped.

Down she plunged into the abyss. But her momentum hurled her against the face of the cliff and she threw out a hand and grabbed hold of the grass growing along the top. A thick clump of grass in each hand, like the hair on a giant's head.

And slowly, every so slowly, she pulled herself up until she was lying on solid ground.

It was only then that she remembered it was Kobal's favourite expression – *Let's do it*.

And then she felt the cold again, the cold icy rain, clawing at her with its skeletal fingers, gnawing at her with its sharp teeth, eating into flesh and bone, and she knew that unless she found shelter and warmth, and in the next few minutes, she would die.

After all she had been through, she would still die.